LAST MAN STANDING

Fargo threw himself off the bed and onto the floor. He heard the rifle boom and then he was rolling. He drew the Colt and thumbed back the hammer. Kroenig's rifle blasted again, into the floor. Fargo came to a stop on his back and fired at Kroenig's chest, but just as he stroked the trigger Kroenig raised the rifle and the slug struck the barrel. The force knocked the rifle from Kroenig's hands. Kroenig bent to snatch it up but Fargo was already rising and caught him across the head with the Colt's barrel. Kroenig tottered. Fargo balled his left fist and drove it into Kroenig's gut. Kroenig sagged and gasped and Fargo let loose with an uppercut that started down around his knees. He nearly broke his knuckles but it was worth it. Kroenig rose onto his toes, took a lurching side step, and keeled facedown with a splat.

THE TRAILSMAN

#353

BITTERROOT BULLETS

by

Jon Sharpe

A SIGNET BOOK

SIGNET
Published by New American Library, a division of
Penguin Group (USA) Inc., 375 Hudson Street,
New York, New York 10014, USA
Penguin Group (Canada), 90 Eglinton Avenue East, Suite 700, Toronto,
Ontario M4P 2Y3, Canada (a division of Pearson Penguin Canada Inc.)
Penguin Books Ltd., 80 Strand, London WC2R 0RL, England
Penguin Ireland, 25 St. Stephen's Green, Dublin 2,
Ireland (a division of Penguin Books Ltd.)
Penguin Group (Australia), 250 Camberwell Road, Camberwell, Victoria 3124,
Australia (a division of Pearson Australia Group Pty. Ltd.)
Penguin Books India Pvt. Ltd., 11 Community Centre, Panchsheel Park,
New Delhi - 110 017, India
Penguin Group (NZ), 67 Apollo Drive, Rosedale, North Shore 0632,
New Zealand (a division of Pearson New Zealand Ltd.)
Penguin Books (South Africa) (Pty.) Ltd., 24 Sturdee Avenue,
Rosebank, Johannesburg 2196, South Africa

Penguin Books Ltd., Registered Offices:
80 Strand, London WC2R 0RL, England

First published by Signet, an imprint of New American Library,
a division of Penguin Group (USA) Inc.

First Printing, March 2011
10 9 8 7 6 5 4 3 2 1

The first chapter of this book previously appeared in *Texas Tangle,* the three hundred
fifty-second volume in this series.

The Trailsman

Beginnings . . . they bend the tree and they mark the man. Skye Fargo was born when he was eighteen. Terror was his midwife, vengeance his first cry. Killing spawned Skye Fargo, ruthless, cold-blooded murder. Out of the acrid smoke of gunpowder still hanging in the air, he rose, cried out a promise never forgotten.

The Trailsman they began to call him all across the West: searcher, scout, hunter, the man who could see where others only looked, his skills for hire but not his soul, the man who lived each day to the fullest, yet trailed each tomorrow. Skye Fargo, the Trailsman, the seeker who could take the wildness of a land and the wanting of a woman and make them his own.

The mountains of western Montana, 1861—where only the brave dare venture, and few who do ever come out again.

1

The trading post was on a stream that fed into the Musselshell River. Skye Fargo had been there before. In addition to supplies, the owner sold whiskey, and Fargo was hankering for a bottle of red-eye. He thumped the counter and paid and took a corner table, as was his habit, with his back to the wall.

At another table four men were playing cards. Three wore buckskins like Fargo. Unlike him, they didn't have his habit of bathing now and then and they stunk to high heaven of hides and guts and sweat. The fourth man wore a suit and a bowler.

Besides the owner there was a kid sweeping the floor. The kid kept glancing at Fargo.

A big man, broad at the shoulder and lean at the hips, Fargo was used to being stared at. He had a Colt on his hip and a splash of vanity at his throat in the form of a red bandanna. As he opened the bottle and poured, he heard an oath from the other table and one of the hide hunters smacked his dirty hand down.

"That's the third in a row, you son of a bitch. You better not be cheating."

The man in the bowler raked in his winnings, saying, "I don't need to cheat, friend. They don't call me Lucky Ed for nothing."

Fargo opened the Monongahela and filled his glass to the brim. He sniffed it, smiled, and emptied the glass in a swallow, then sat back as the liquor warmed him all over. He was tipping the bottle again when two women came out of the back. Right away his interest perked.

One was older than the other by a considerable number of years but both were easy on the eyes. The oldest had black hair; the youngest was a redhead. Their dresses swelled nicely at their bosoms and hips. Their ruby lips were spread in warm smiles.

"Well, now," said the oldest, who had to be in her thirties, as she stopped at Fargo's table. "What do we have here?"

"He's awful handsome," the youngest said. She looked to be all of eighteen, if that.

"Ladies," Fargo said, and devoured them with his eyes. "Why don't you join me?"

"Don't mind if we do," said the oldest. She winked at the young one and they pulled out chairs. "I'm Brianna. This here is Calypso."

"Calypso?" Fargo said. It was a new one on him.

"My ma got it out of a book," Calypso said. "She thought it had a pretty sound."

Fargo raised an arm and caught the owner's attention and pointed at the women. The owner nodded and promptly brought over two more glasses.

"Don't forget we have other customers," he said to the women as he set the glasses down.

Brianna glanced over her shoulder and frowned. "I'd rather not, Tom. They get awful rough."

"It's your job," Tom said.

"Not to be beat, it ain't," Brianna said.

"The last time all Kroenig did was slap you," Tom persisted.

"Six times." Brianna held her ground. "My cheek was swollen for a week."

"I'll protect you," Tom said.

"That's what you said last time."

"Damn it, Bri—"

Fargo looked at him and drummed his fingers on the table. Tom noticed, and swallowed heavily.

"Sorry. We shouldn't squabble in front of you, should we?"

"Well now," Brianna said as Tom walked off, "that was interesting. All you did was stare at him and he tucked tail."

"Tom knows me," Fargo said. He filled their glasses and took a sip from his own.

Brianna placed her elbows on the table and her chin in her hands and studied him. "Tom Carson ain't a kitten. What makes you so special that he treats you with so much respect? You don't look mean so it must be something else."

"You look handsome," Calypso made a point of saying again.

To change the subject Fargo asked, "You ladies worked here long?"

"Going on a couple of months," Brianna replied.

"You don't sound happy about it."

"We're not. There's not enough trade to keep us busy. I am bored half the time and there's nothing I hate worse in this world than being bored."

"I hate runny noses," Calypso said.

Brianna had more to complain about. "When Tom hired us he made it sound better here than it is. Claimed we'd make a hundred dollars a month, easy. Hell, we're lucky if we make half that much."

"Why do you stay?"

"We agreed to stick for half a year and I'm a woman of my word."

"Nice body, too."

Brianna chuckled and reached across and put her hand on his. "I am commencing to like you. Do you plan to stay the night?"

"If he is we should flip a coin," Calypso said. "I like him too."

"What about them?" Fargo said with a nod at the other table.

"They can play with themselves for all I care." Brianna said it too loudly.

All three buffalo men shifted in their chairs and the largest got up and came over.

"Were you talkin' about us, whore?"

"Leave me be, Kroenig," Brianna said.

"I don't believe I will," Kroenig declared, and grabbed her arm.

2

Brianna tried to pull free but Kroenig was much too strong.

"Let go, damn you."

"What was that about playing with ourselves?"

"I was talking about someone else," Brianna lied. Her face was contorted in pain. "You're hurting me."

Kroenig bent down. "I'll hurt you more if you don't quit sassin' me." He pulled her partway to her feet. "I want you to sit in my lap until I'm done with cards and then you and me will go in the back."

"I don't want to sit in your lap."

"You're a whore. You do what I want you to do."

"The lady is with me," Fargo said.

Kroenig barely glanced at him. "This don't concern you, mister. Keep your mouth shut or I'll come around and shut it for you."

"Don't bother," Fargo said. "I'll come around to you."

And he was out of his chair and drawing his Colt before Kroenig could blink. He smashed it against Kroenig's temple and the big man staggered but didn't go down. Fargo slammed it against him again and Kroenig folded and lay still, save for a slight shaking of his fingers.

Kroenig's friends were rooted in disbelief. Then one of them started to rise and the other pushed his chair back. They stopped when Fargo leveled the Colt.

"I wouldn't."

"He's our pard," the filthiest rumbled, "and you hit him."

"He's a jackass," Fargo said. "Pick him up and drag him out and don't come back until after I leave."

"You can't make us go if we don't want to."

Fargo cocked the Colt. "Care to bet?"

They looked at one another and the filthiest said, "Who in hell do you think you are?"

"Me," Fargo said, and fired into the floor between them.

Both jumped, and the filthy one stood. He had a wide leather belt around his waist and a Starr revolver tucked under it. He splayed his fingers as if to reach for it but didn't. "You're makin' me mad, mister."

"Ease your hardware out and put it on the table." Fargo wagged his Colt at the other one. "You too. You can collect them in the morning."

"I'll be damned if I'll let you disarm us," the filthy one told him.

"You ain't got the right," the other said.

"No, I don't," Fargo said. "But there you have it." He had run into their kind before. Given half a chance, they'd pay him back for hurting their friend, any way they could. "Shed or chuck lead. Your choice."

"I won't forget you for this," the filthy one growled. Using two fingers he plucked the revolver and set it down.

"Me either," said the other, doing the same.

Fargo covered them as they gripped Kroenig by the arms and went to drag him. "Wait. Roll him over."

The filthy one did.

Kroenig didn't have a revolver, just a big skinning knife in a beaded sheath.

"Off you go," Fargo said.

"Armitage," the filthy one said.

Fargo looked at him.

"That's my handle. Remember it so when I buck you out in gore you'll know who did it." Armitage waited as if expecting Fargo to say who he was.

"Today would be nice," Fargo said.

Muttering, Armitage and the other man hauled Kroenig out into the gray of twilight.

"Well, hell," said the man in the bowler. "There goes my card winnings for tonight."

Fargo twirled the Colt into his holster and reclaimed his seat. He emptied his glass and tipped the bottle to his cup.

"Now where were we, ladies?"

"You took a terrible chance," Brianna said. "Armitage and Lester love to beat on folks almost as much as they love to drink."

"They'll jump you when you least expect," Calypso predicted. "You'd best grow eyes in the back of your head."

"I already did." Fargo topped off both of their glasses and raised his. "How about a toast?"

"To what?" Brianna asked.

"To a night we won't soon forget."

"You don't care, do you?" Calypso said. "You're not scared even a little bit."

"I don't do yellow," Fargo said.

"I knew a man like you once," Brianna said. "Proud. Stubborn. He never backed down to anyone. Then one morning they found him in an alley with five or six bullet holes in his back."

"I get the point."

"I hope so, and I hope you take heed," Brianna said. "Because if you don't you'll wind up very dead."

3

They tossed a coin and much to Brianna's disappointment, Calypso won. Her room was small but comfortable—a bed, a chest of drawers, a small rug. Pink curtains were over the window. She closed the door and leaned against it and smiled almost shyly. "Lucky me."

Fargo couldn't quite get a read on her. She'd been quiet most of the evening. "Care for some?" he asked, and shook the whiskey bottle. There was about a third left.

"I don't much like coffin varnish, to tell the truth," Calypso said. "Makes my head hurt."

Fargo shrugged and chugged and smacked his lips.

"I can't get over how handsome you are."

"So you keep saying."

Calypso fussed with her red curls and then with her dress and bit her lower lip.

"Something the matter?"

"I don't know what to do."

About to chug more whiskey, Fargo peered at her over the bottle. "You take off your clothes. I take off mine. We have fun. It's not complicated."

"No, not that." Calypso laughed and bit her lips again. "You're only about my twentieth and I guess I'm still green at this."

Fargo straightened. "Brianna said you've been at this two months here."

"There haven't been that many in those two months," Calypso said. "And it's only those two. Before this, I wasn't a whore. I only came with her because I was desperate for money."

"Hell," Fargo said.

"I'm from Ohio. Small-town girl. I married a boy named Wesley. He was so sweet. He was always saying as how we would have a fine house and kids and everything. He took me to Saint Louis and from there we went to Denver and that's where the horse kicked him in the head and he died."

"Hell," Fargo said again.

Calypso gestured. "I didn't know what to do. I was broke. I didn't have any skills to speak of. I'm not much of a cook and I can't sew for beans. So I started asking around at the saloons and I met Brianna and she mentioned as how she knew a fella who was looking for girls to come work at his trading post and here I am."

"Lucky me," Fargo said dryly.

"I'm sorry I'm so awkward at this," Calypso said. "Thing is, I'm not sure I'm cut out for it. I don't much like being pawed by men I don't care for."

"I'll go find Brianna." Fargo reached for the latch but she stayed his hand.

"Oh, no. Please. Stay."

"It's no bother," Fargo said.

"I'd rather it was you than those hunters," Calypso said. "They stink and their breath is so bad, when they kiss me I have to hold my own."

"There's the gambler."

"Lucky Ed? He passes through now and then but he never

pays for pokes. I think he has a wife somewhere." Calypso tightened her grip on his wrist and pressed against him. "I'll get down on my knees if I have to."

"To beg me or the other?" Fargo asked with a grin.

"What? Oh. Not that." Calypso reddened. "To ask you to stay. I expect it will be nice with a man like you." She rose on her toes and kissed him on the lips, a quick peck with no passion. "There. See?"

Fargo smothered a laugh. "Girl, if your heart's not in this then—"

"I know, I know. But I have to eat. And I told Mr. Carson I'd stick, just like Brianna."

"You gave your word and you aim to keep it." A trait Fargo admired since he did the same.

"Yes," Calypso said. "I did."

Fargo turned and sat on the bed and took another healthy swallow. "The twentieth, you say?"

"Maybe the fifteenth. I haven't kept count." Calypso wrung her hands. "Don't tell Mr. Carson but Brianna takes most of them to spare me. She's real nice, giving me time to break in, as she puts it."

"You and a horse," Fargo said.

"Pardon?"

Fargo patted the bed. "We can do this or not. But if we do, I don't aim to spend all night at it."

"Oh." Calypso came to the bed in small steps and primly sat at the end of it. "How's this?"

"You sure know how to get a man excited."

"No," Calypso said. "I don't. That's part of the problem. I mean, I did it a lot of times with Wesley. But mostly he did the doing and I just laid there."

"Ah," Fargo said.

"What does that mean?"

"Just 'Ah,'" Fargo answered.

Calypso fiddled with her curls some more, and smiled. She had a nice smile. "Brianna has been teaching me some tricks. I can try one she says always works."

"Does it involve talking?"

"Goodness, no. She says a girl shouldn't do all that much jabbering. That we should get to it and pleasure the man and then shoo him out and forget him."

"A gal after my own heart," Fargo said.

"You don't want to remember me?" Calypso asked, sounding hurt.

"I doubt I can forget you now," Fargo said. "When it comes to priming the pump, you beat all."

"Is that a good thing or a bad thing?"

"Priming is good if you know how to do it."

"Do you?"

Fargo coughed. "I've had a little experience. Why?"

"I was thinking maybe you could do the priming and it would go a lot easier."

"I'm all for easy," Fargo said.

4

Fargo was having second thoughts. He'd pulled Calypso to him and kissed her and fondled her yet she still sat there as stiff as a board, her lips so tight together it would take a pry bar to open them. Finally he sat back. "The priming won't work if you don't help."

"I'm a little scared."

"Were you scared with the others?"

"Oh, Lord, yes. More scared than I am with you."

"How did they get your legs apart?"

"Pardon."

"Nothing," Fargo said. He leaned his back to the wall and let her place her head on his chest and stroked her hair. "This is going to take a while."

"I'm sorry." Calypso closed her eyes and tiny tears formed in their corners.

"Tell me you're not going to cry."

"I might," Calypso said, and sniffled.

"What the hell for?"

"Because I like you and I want you to like me. I should be more relaxed with you but for some reason I'm not." She opened her eyes and dabbed at the corners with a finger. "I'm a mess, aren't I?"

"A pretty mess," Fargo said, and rubbed her shoulders. He felt some of the stiffness go out of her.

"Do you really think I'm pretty?"

"Wouldn't have said so if I didn't." Fargo ran his hand down the middle of her back and up again.

She grinned and shivered slightly. "I like that."

"It's good you like something." Fargo roved lower and she immediately tensed up so he went back to rubbing above her waist.

"My ma used to say that we like things better when we have to work for them."

Fargo had to laugh. "In that case I'll like you more than any woman I've ever slept with."

"Have there been a lot?"

"Like you, I haven't counted them."

"I bet there has," Calypso said. "A handsome man like you, women would fall over themselves to be with you."

"You're not falling," Fargo said.

Calypso twisted her head up. "Inside I am. I just have a hard time showing it. It was the same with Wesley. It's why he had to do the priming."

Fargo kissed her left eyebrow and then her right and then nipped lightly at her earlobe.

Calypso giggled. "You sure are playful."

"I'm horny," Fargo said. Lightly clasping her chin, he pressed his mouth to hers. He was careful not to press too hard or try to use his tongue. Gradually, she responded. Her lips loosened and her body relaxed and she timidly ran a hand through his hair under his hat. When he sat back she grinned.

"That was real nice."

"It gets better."

"Thank you for being so patient with me. Most of those other men I've been with wanted to get it over with and be on their way."

"Might be best not to talk about them," Fargo said.

"Oh. Sorry. It must make you uncomfortable, thinking about other men who have had me."

Not at all, Fargo thought. He just wanted her to shut up.

He kissed her again and this time he roamed his hand from her shoulder down her side to her belly. He felt her flutter through the dress. He would have gone lower but she pressed her forehead to his neck. "What now?" he asked.

"You're making me hot."

"That's the whole point."

"Hot all over," Calypso said. "Hot like I used to be with Wesley. With the others I mostly felt cold."

"There you go again."

"Sorry. I won't talk again until it's over."

Fargo had his doubts but she proved as good as her word. For a long while he caressed and fondled and stroked until she was on her back with her arms around his neck and hunger in her eyes. Her body softened and she spread her legs. He didn't go there just yet. He took his time removing her dress and her chemise. Naked, she was beautiful: soft, creamy skin, small but full breasts, thighs that went on forever. He drank in her loveliness. Pressing his mouth to her throat, he licked between her breasts and across her belly to her bush. She gasped and wriggled and dug her nails into his arms.

Fargo sat up and reached for his buckle to undo his gun belt.

That was when the door burst open and in strode Kroenig with a rifle in his hands and hate in his eyes. The left side of his face was swollen and discolored. "I've got you now, you son of a bitch."

5

Fargo threw himself off the bed and onto the floor. He heard the rifle boom and Calypso say, "Oh!" Then he was rolling and as he rolled he drew the Colt and thumbed back the hammer. Kroenig's rifle blasted again, into the floor. Fargo came to a stop on his back and fired at Kroenig's chest, but just as he stroked the trigger Kroenig raised the rifle and the slug struck the barrel. The force knocked the rifle from Kroenig's hands. Kroenig bent to snatch it up but Fargo was already rising and caught him across the head with the Colt's barrel. Kroenig tottered. Fargo balled his left fist and drove it into Kroenig's gut. Kroenig sagged and gasped and Fargo let loose with an uppercut that started down around his knees. He nearly broke his knuckles but it was worth it. Kroenig rose onto his toes, took a lurching side step, and keeled facedown with a splat.

Fargo pointed the Colt. "I should blow out your wick."

"Skye?" Calypso said.

"In a minute." Fargo holstered the Colt and laid hold of the back of Kroenig's buckskin shirt to haul him from the room.

"Now would be better."

Something in her voice made Fargo turn. "Damn," he said, and was to the bed in a bound. She was on her side, looking dazed, blood trickling from a hole high on her right shoulder.

"Lie still." He leaned over her and saw the exit wound, twice as big and leaking twice as much blood.

"I'm sorry," Calypso said.

"For what?"

"Being such a bother. I started to sit up and he shot and I was hit."

Feet pounded in the hall. Into the room rushed Brianna. Behind her were Tom Carson and Lucky Ed. Brianna took in the situation at a glance and came to the bed and clasped Calypso's hand.

"Tom, we'll need hot water and bandages. A whole lot of bandages."

Carson was glowering at Kroenig. "Damn him. He must have snuck in the back."

"The bandages, Tom," Brianna said.

Lucky Ed, who was ogling Brianna's fanny as she bent over the bed, blocked Carson's way.

"Get the hell out of here," Fargo said.

The gambler glanced at Kroenig and at Fargo's Colt and prudently backed away.

Brianna shifted Calypso onto her side and smoothed her hair. "Poor baby. How do you feel?"

"Weak," Calypso said. "Dizzy."

With a nod at Kroenig, Brianna said to Fargo, "Was it his shot or yours?"

"His."

"Is he dead, I hope?"

"No."

"Get the bastard out, would you? Don't worry about Calypso. I'll take care of her. I've treated gunshots before."

"If you need help," Fargo said. He had tended to more than his share, too.

"I won't but thanks for the offer."

Fargo dragged Kroenig out and down the hall to the back door. Behind the trading post a small hill rose to a higher hill and beyond that were more. He dragged Kroenig around the corner to the stream. Kroenig groaned and stirred. Stepping back, Fargo kicked him in the ribs hard enough to crack a few and sent him tumbling down the bank into the water. The splash sent spray every which way.

Kroenig sputtered and coughed and rose to his hands and knees spitting water. He looked about in confusion and then clutched his side and swore. He started to crawl out and saw Fargo. His hand flew to the knife on his hip.

"I wish you'd try," Fargo said.

Kroenig moved his hand away from the hilt. "No," he said, and coughed. "I won't give you an excuse."

"You already have," Fargo said. "You shot the girl."

"Calypso?" Kroenig shook his head. "Like hell. I was aiming at you."

"You're a piss-poor shot."

"You moved."

"Damn right I did."

"Shoot me, then, damn you," Kroenig snapped. "Get it over with."

Fargo was sorely tempted. It would have been so easy. Draw and core his brain and that would be that. But all the man had was a knife and he was making no move to use it.

"I'm sorry about her," Kroenig said. "She's a good gal. Shy as hell and lousy in bed but a good gal."

"You couldn't let it be," Fargo said.

"Mister, you damn near busted my head open. And all because I wanted that whore to sit on my lap." Kroenig jabbed a finger at him. "What did you expect me to do? Go slinking off? If that gal is hurt bad, you're as much to blame as me."

"I didn't squeeze the trigger," Fargo said. Suddenly wheeling, he made for the building.

"Wait! I want my rifle."

"Go to hell." Fargo went around the corner and slammed the door shut after him.

"This ain't over, mister!" Kroenig hollered. "You hear me? This ain't over."

"No," Fargo said to himself. "It's not."

6

Fargo was slumped in a chair at the corner table nursing a second bottle. It had been almost an hour since Calypso had been shot and he was still waiting for word on how she was faring. Tom Carson was in the back with Brianna. He glared at the entrance, half hoping Kroenig would make another attempt on his life.

Over at the other table Lucky Ed was playing solitaire. He happened to look up and said, "Hey, mister. Care for a game? Just you and me?"

"No."

"We don't have to play for money if you don't want to."

"No."

"I just want something to do."

"No means no."

"What harm can it do? There are just you and me. A friendly game for a few hours. What do you say?"

Fargo switched his glare from the entrance to the gambler.

"I say that if you ask me that one more goddamn time, I'll give you a taste of what I gave Kroenig."

Lucky Ed blinked. "It's the girl, isn't it? You're taking her being shot sort of personal, aren't you?"

"I take everything personal," Fargo said. "Now play your cards and leave me be."

Lucky Ed shrugged and clammed up. He had been wrong about one thing—Fargo and he weren't the only ones there. As Fargo raised the bottle, the kid with the broom came over.

"Can I talk to you, mister?"

"No."

"It's really important."

"Doesn't anyone around here listen worth a damn?" Fargo grumbled. As if his day wasn't bad enough, he was beginning to get a headache.

"I want to hire you."

Fargo looked at him. The kid was scrawny and had peach fuzz on his chin. In addition to an apron he wore an old shirt much too big and baggy britches. "*You* want to hire *me*?"

"Yes, sir."

"To do what?"

"Mr. Carson tells me that you're a scout. One of the best, he says. He says you can track as good as an Apache and you can shoot a fly off a post at a hundred yards and you've killed a heap of men, red and white."

"Mr. Carson talks too damn much. Go away." Fargo drank more rotgut. When he put down the bottle the kid was still there. "I am beginning to hate this place."

"I want to be a scout like you," the boy said.

"Do you, now?" Fargo replied. "Here's how you do it." He leaned his forearms on the table. "Your family gets wiped out. You have no one in the world but you. You go to the frontier and take up with an old-timer who teaches you a lot and then you live with the Sioux a spell and they teach you a whole lot more and then you become friends with a scout who teaches you what little you don't already know and then you're a scout yourself."

"Or I could hire you to teach me," the kid said.

"No, you couldn't."

"I have forty dollars. It's all I have in the whole world and it's yours if you'll teach me."

"Forty dollars for all I know?" Fargo shook his head. "Go find some dust to sweep."

"It's important to me," the kid persisted. "I want it more than I've ever wanted anything." He paused. "Hasn't something ever been that important to you?"

"Right now being left alone is important."

"It would mean the world to me."

Fargo looked at him. The kid had an earnest face with freckles on his cheeks and nose, and green, trusting eyes. "Listen, kid—"

"My name is Pete but everybody calls me Petey. Petey Evans, that's me."

"Petey," Fargo said. "I scout now and then but I do other things and at the moment I'm doing other things. Go to a fort. Find a scout on the army's payroll and ask him to take you on as a helper. It'll take you a few years but you might become a real scout one day."

"But you're here now," Petey said. "And you're not doing much but trying to get drunk."

"Everyone wants to piss me off today," Fargo said.

"Please," Petey said. He reached under his apron and fumbled at a pocket and produced a handful of crumpled bills and coins, which he placed on the table. "Here it is. All I have. How much of your time will it buy me?"

"Hey, Petey," Lucky Ed called over. "Want to play some cards? Five-card stud, just you and me?"

"No, Mr. Bishop, but thank you." Petey didn't take his eyes off of Fargo.

"You don't know what you're asking," Fargo told him. "Being a scout is more than learning how to track and shoot. It's learning how to survive."

"All I'm asking is that you give me my forty dollars' worth," Petey said. "The important stuff I need to know. I'll take it from there."

"What do your folks say about this?"

Petey grew downcast and averted his gaze. "They're dead. I have kin back east but I never met them but a few times when I was little and I doubt they care much what happens to me."

"Put the money back in your pocket."

"You won't do it?" Petey looked fit to cry.

"I couldn't spare more than a few days," Fargo said. "That's not nearly enough to teach you all you'd need to know."

"I'm an awful fast learner. Teach me what you can and I'll be happy."

"You're not listening. The little I could teach you won't make a scout of you. It might only get you dead if you go off and convince the army to hire you."

"I'm willing to take that chance."

"When I was your age I didn't much care whether I lived or died, either," Fargo said.

"Oh. It's not that. I want to live. I want to live more than anything," Petey said. "I have a goal in my life and it's important to me."

"Even if I could spare a week that's not nearly long enough."

"It would be a week's worth more than I know now." Petey pushed the money closer. "Please. I'm begging you."

Fargo emptied the bottle in a gulp and set it to one side and picked up the bills. "There doesn't happen to be a mule around here anywhere, does there?"

"What? No, sir. Why?"

"I could use a good swift kick."

Petey became a second sun, grinning from ear to ear. "Does this mean you will?"

"It means I'm an idiot and you have yourself a teacher."

7

The kid was eager—Fargo would say that for him. He'd pitched camp in a stand of pines where his fire wouldn't be spotted by unfriendly eyes, and the kid showed up at the crack of dawn as he had told him to.

Fargo was pouring his second cup of coffee and had to grin at the tousle-headed bundle of bones who stood there impatient to begin. "What did Carson say about you taking the day off?"

"I didn't take it off. I quit."

"Hell, boy," Fargo said. "What are you going to do for a living after I go?"

"I have plans," Petey said, but he didn't go into them. He had been holding his left arm behind his back and now he brought it around holding a small knapsack.

"What's that?" Fargo asked.

"All I own in the world." Petey looked about them. "So, will we live here for the next week or move around some?"

"You want to camp with me?"

Petey nodded. "It's only a week, and I aim to spend every minute at your side."

Fargo wasn't sure he liked that idea. "I never said you could be my shadow."

"You didn't say I couldn't." Petey gestured. "I won't be a

nuisance. I promise. I just need to learn every little bit you can teach me."

Fargo sipped and debated whether to go through with it or give the kid his money back. "Are those the only clothes you have?"

Petey held up the knapsack. "I have a spare shirt but it's got a hole in it and I don't have any thread or a needle to mend it."

"Do you have a revolver?"

"No."

"A rifle?"

"No."

"Do you have a damn knife?"

"No."

"Those shoes your only footwear?"

"Yes."

"You don't even own a pair of boots?"

"I'd do this in my bare feet if I had to."

Fargo set his tin cup down and drew his Colt. Unloading it, he stood. He twirled the Colt forward and twirled it back and flipped it into the air and caught it smoothly by the handles and twirled it into his holster with a flourish.

"Goodness gracious," Petey said.

Fargo drew it again and handed it to him and Petey took it in both hands as if afraid he would drop it. "Ever handled a pistol?"

"No, sir. I never even so much as touched one."

"Hell," Fargo said. "Hold it in one hand. Get used to the feel. Cock it a few times and let down the hammer nice and easy."

Petey applied his thumb to the hammer and it clicked. "I won't break it, will I?"

"Listen to me," Fargo said, and put his hand on the kid's shoulder. "We can't do this if you're going to be stupid. It's made of metal, for God's sake. You can beat somebody over the head and it won't break."

"Like you did to Mr. Kroenig." Petey cocked it and pointed it and closed his left eye and stuck the tip of his tongue between his lips.

"What the hell are you doing?"

"Aiming."

"You take that long and you'll be dead before you can squint." Fargo took the Colt. He reloaded and shoved it into his holster. Ten feet away was a pine with a knot about as big as his hand. "See there?" Fluidly drawing, he fanned a shot from the hip and put the slug smack in the center of the knot.

"God in heaven," Petey said. "Could I ever be that good?"

"Depends on how much you practice." Fargo held the pistol out. "Your turn. Don't try to fan it like I did. Hold it in both hands and point. And keep your damn tongue in your mouth. You look like a jackass with it sticking out."

"Oh. Sorry. I do that when I concentrate real hard."

"Cock the pistol and sight down the barrel and when you're ready, squeeze the trigger. Don't jerk it. Don't pull on it. Squeeze nice and slow." Fargo demonstrated with his finger.

"You didn't do that when you shot."

"Yes, I did, only I squeezed fast. Now pay attention and do like I told you."

Petey took deliberate aim. He started to poke his tongue out, caught himself, and said, "I'm ready."

"Why are your shoulders hunched?"

"I do that when I'm nervous."

"Relax. Line up the front sight with the knot and take a deep breath and hold the Colt steady."

Petey sucked air into his lungs and became a statue.

"Fire."

The slug not only missed the knot; it missed the tree.

"Dang," Petey said.

Fargo sighed. "This is going to take a while."

8

Being eager wasn't always enough. As Fargo soon discovered, Petey Evans had no knack for the skills it took to be a scout. No knack whatsoever. The kid had five thumbs on each hand. He was so awkward and clumsy that by the second day Fargo was tempted to give the money back and tell him to stick to sweeping floors.

At the moment they were practicing how to mount a horse. Petey, it turned out, didn't own one. He had come to the trading post on a supply wagon, and stayed.

"Your animal is awful big," the kid said as he gripped the saddle horn and hooked his foot in the stirrup. With a grunt he swung up but he misjudged and almost sat on the saddle horn and not the saddle. Sliding back, he wriggled and said, "They ought to make these things more comfortable."

"You'll get used to it," Fargo said. "Scouts sometimes have to ride ten hours or more a day."

"That would kill my backside. I wouldn't be able to sit down for a month of Sundays."

Fargo had him lift the reins and adjust his posture, then told him to ride in a small circle.

"Easy as pie," Petey said, and practically shouted, "Go, horse, go!"

The Ovaro stood there.

"What's the matter with it? Why won't it move when I want it to?"

"Use your heels," Fargo said.

Petey slammed his legs against the stallion and it exploded into motion. Squawking in surprise, he gripped the reins too far forward. A tree loomed and he shifted his weight as if to make the Ovaro turn and instead a low limb caught him across the chest and sent him tumbling. He lay on his back with the breath knocked out of him and saw Fargo looking down.

"What did I do wrong?"

"Practically everything."

"I used my heels like you said to."

"No, you used your legs." Fargo grasped Petey's arm and pulled him to his feet. "All it takes is a tap. And when you want to turn you use the reins. You don't lean to the right or the left."

"Your horse must be dumb. Other horses would have figured it out."

"My horse is smarter than you," Fargo said. "When you climb on one, you're in charge. Most horses are used to doing things a certain way. You don't make it up as you go."

Again and again Fargo had him mount and ride in a circle. Most of the time Petey reined too sharply or not sharply enough. Once he nearly rode the stallion into a pine. Another time, as he was climbing back on, he hooked his foot in the stirrup and started to pull himself up, only to slip and lose his hold and fall upside down onto his shoulders.

"Has that ever happened to you?" he asked as he brushed himself off.

"Not in this life."

"You're poking fun at me, I can tell." Petey stepped to

the stallion and wrapped his hands around the saddle horn again.

"But I'm going to keep at this if it kills me."

"It just might," Fargo said.

By the end of the third day the kid could ride without flouncing and use the reins well enough to thread through the trees almost at a trot.

"Are you watching?" he crowed.

"Don't get cocky."

Next they practiced throwing Fargo's Arkansas toothpick.

Fargo could stick it in a stump ten times out of ten. Petey, even after an hour, could do it once in every twenty throws.

"What am I doing wrong?"

"Besides not holding it right and letting go too soon and throwing all wrong?"

Petey frowned and whipped his arm a few times. "Be patient with me, will you? This doesn't come as easy as I thought it would."

"It's your week," Fargo said.

"When do I learn to track? I want to learn that more than anything."

"So you can have venison in your supper pot?" Fargo said.

"The game I have in mind is a heap more dangerous."

Fargo glanced at him. "Leave the bears and the buffalo to those who know what they're doing."

It was impossible to impart every nuance of the scouting craft in the time they had. Fargo stuck to the basics: the way to tell how old a track was, how to gauge the gait and sometimes whether the animal was male or female, tracks to fight shy of, like grizzly prints, and more.

Petey absorbed it like a sponge absorbed water. He did have a good eye for details. His questions were sometimes unexpected. At one point he brought up, "How do I tell the difference between a dog print and a coyote or a wolf?"

"In all my time as a scout I've hardly ever had to track dogs," Fargo said.

"Tell me anyway. How do I tell when the dog is about the same size as a wolf?"

Fargo sketched in the dirt with a stick, showing how a dog's tracks tended to be rounder and how usually the pads were set farther apart than on a wolf's or a coyote's.

"Any other differences?"

Fargo shrugged. "Dogs tend to wander all over the place while coyotes and wolves tend to go in straight lines for long spells."

"Ever had to kill a dog?" Petey asked.

"A few."

"What's the best way? Shoot it in the heart or the lungs or maybe blow a leg off and club it to death?"

"The best way to kill anything is to shoot it in the head," Fargo said. "Why do you ask? You fixing to kill a dog or two?"

"I was just curious. Haven't you ever been curious about anything?"

"All the time," Fargo said. And he was becoming very curious, indeed, about Petey Evans.

9

The black of night had spread across the Musselshell country. Stars sparkled like so many fireflies. Coyotes commenced to yip, and in the pines an owl hooted.

Fargo sat at the fire sipping coffee. Across from him, Petey had his chin in his hands and was gazing sadly into the fire.

"Something wrong?"

"I only have three days left."

"You're doing fine," Fargo said, which wasn't quite the truth. The kid was fair. Not good, not bad, just fair. And to be a scout, a competent scout, a person had to be better than fair.

"I'm trying my best."

"Maybe you'll decide to do something else with your life," Fargo said. "You never know."

"I know I need to do this. I just wish I'd done it a year ago."

"You're young yet. You have plenty of time."

Petey looked up. There was an odd glint in his eyes. "No, Mr. Fargo. I don't."

"How old are you, anyhow?" Fargo hadn't bothered to ask because it wasn't important.

"Fourteen," Petey said, almost defiantly.

"I repeat. You have plenty of time."

"That's not how life works. I've learned the hard way that

if you don't do what you want to do or need to do when you want or need to do it, life can see to it that you never do."

"Mind explaining that?" Fargo said.

Just then the Ovaro raised its head and nickered. Fargo swiveled and placed his hand on the Colt but before he could draw Kroenig stepped out of the darkness with a rifle trained on him and grim menace on his face.

"Don't even think it."

"You stupid son of a bitch," Fargo said.

"Take your hand off that six-shooter."

With the muzzle of Kroenig's buffalo gun fixed on him, Fargo had no choice.

Kroenig came to within a few yards. He wagged the rifle. "Not so stupid that I couldn't make Tom Carson give my gun back. He claimed he didn't know what you did with it. But I saw you ride off and you didn't have it so I figured you hid it at the trading post and told him not to give it to me." Kroenig grinned. "Pretty smart, huh?"

Fargo probed the darkness for movement. "Where are your pards?"

"They didn't want any part of this. They said I was being foolish. They said I should drop it."

"They were right."

Kroenig already had the hammer back and his finger was curled around the trigger. "Some things a man can't drop and still call himself a man."

Petey showed surprising backbone. He straightened and said angrily, "Go away, consarn you. I've hired him and I won't have you killing him and spoiling everything."

"Hired him for what, boy?" Kroenig asked without looking at him.

"He's teaching me how to be a scout."

"You?" Kroenig laughed. "Boy, you'd make about as good

a scout as I would one of them who does sums and such. I ain't got a head for arithmetic and you ain't got a head, period."

"Don't insult me," Petey said.

"Besides," Kroenig went on, "I don't aim to kill him."

"Then what?" Petey said.

"He's beat on me twice. I'm going to repay the favor, only worse."

"I'll be a witness," Petey said. "I could report you to the law."

"What law?" Kroenig rejoined. "There ain't any for a thousand miles. And were you fixing to report him for beating on me?" His voice hardened. "Shut the hell up and let us men deal with men business."

Fargo held his coffee cup close to his chest. It was still half full. "I'm asking you to let this be."

"You pistol-whipped me, you bastard. No way in hell I'll drop it." Kroenig raised the Sharps to his shoulder. "On your feet and turn around."

"From behind?" Fargo said. "How yellow are you?"

Kroenig sighted down the barrel. "It doesn't have to be a beating. Make me mad enough and I'll blow out your wick, you and the boy, both."

"Hey, now," Petey said, and started to stand.

Kroenig swung the rifle to cover him, growling, "Stay right where you are, boy."

Fargo took a long bound and threw the coffee into Kroenig's eyes. Kroenig tried to aim but for a second he couldn't see and that was all it took for Fargo to draw his Colt and arc it at Kroenig's head. Kroenig threw himself back, blinking frantically to clear his vision, and the Colt only glanced his temple. The Sharps went off, the slug kicking up spurts of flame from the fire. Then Fargo had hold of it and shoved it aside even as he slammed the Colt at Kroenig's head. Kroenig ducked while bellowing, "Not this time!" and then kicked Fargo in the leg. Agony exploded and Fargo's leg buckled. He landed on his back. Kroenig tore the Sharps free, reversed his grip, and raised it like a club. Sheer rage contorted his face.

"Now I have you!" he roared, and tensed to bring the heavy stock crashing down.

Fargo shot him.

Kroenig looked down at the hole in his chest. He didn't fall. Instead, he roared in rage and raised the rifle higher.

Fargo shot him again.

Staggering, Kroenig bleated like a stricken goat. He fell to his knees, incredulity replacing his rage. "Damn you," he said. Pink froth flecked his lips and he pitched forward, dead before he hit the ground.

Grimacing in pain, Fargo rose and began to reload.

Petey was transfixed. "You killed him."

"I sure as hell did."

"You really killed him."

"He was about to bash my brains out," Fargo said, "and I'm partial to breathing."

Petey tore his gaze from Kroenig and beamed his sunshine smile. "You're wonderful."

About to insert a cartridge into the chamber, Fargo paused. "I'm what?"

"You're everything I want to be. Meeting you was the best thing that ever happened to me."

"Hell, boy," Fargo said. "Don't make me out to be special when I'm not."

"You just don't know," Petey Evans said.

10

The next morning they buried the body in a shallow grave.

Fargo stripped it first and rolled the naked hulk into the hole. He folded the buckskins and went into the trees and found Kroenig's sorrel. The rest of the morning he spent teaching Petey about tracking. The sun was straight overhead when they returned to camp.

Fargo put his hands on his hips and said, "I reckon they're not going to show."

"Who?" Petey asked.

"Kroenig's pards. They must have gone their own way, which is good news for you."

"Me?"

Fargo nodded at the sorrel and the folded buckskins with the Sharps on top of them. "It's all yours."

"What is?"

"His stuff. His horse. I don't need any of it." Fargo went over and picked up the Sharps and tossed it to him.

Petey barely got his hands up in time to catch it before it struck him in the chest. He stared at it and then at the horse and the clothes with the expression of a five-year-old experiencing his first Christmas. "You can't be serious."

"A parson once told me that the Almighty works in mysterious ways. I told him that was a pitiful excuse. But you needed a horse and a rifle and clothes and here they are."

"It would be stealing," Petey said, his voice thick with the longing he was trying to deny.

"How can you steal from a dead man? He doesn't have any more use for any of it." Fargo motioned. "Help yourself."

"All mine?" Petey said, and caressed the Sharps as if it were a girl.

"We'll need to cut the buckskins down to fit. I have a needle and thread but I'm not much at sewing."

"The horse too?" Petey timidly patted its neck.

"You're in hog heaven," Fargo said.

"I don't—" Petey stopped and looked away. He bowed his head and his shoulders shook.

"Tell me you're not crying."

"I'm so happy I could bust," Petey said, and broke into loud sobs.

"Oh, hell." Fargo didn't usually have coffee in the middle of the day but he kindled the fire and put the pot on and sat back to wait for the sniveling to stop. He supposed he shouldn't have been surprised. The kid was only fourteen, after all, and boys that age let their feelings get the better of them.

Eventually Petey wiped his sleeve across his face and turned. He sat and examined the Sharps and the buckskins. "There's blood on this shirt. I don't know as I can wear a shirt with someone else's blood on it."

"Blood washes out. Soak it in the stream and pound it with a rock and that should do the trick."

Petey raised adoring eyes. "You're the finest man who ever lived."

"Don't start with that again," Fargo said. "Thank Kroenig, not me. He was the one who didn't know when to leave well enough alone."

"You don't know what this means. Now I can do everything I wanted."

"Be a scout, you mean?"

"That too," Petey said. He suddenly got up and stepped to the sorrel and opened the saddlebags. "Why, look in here."

He commenced to take things out and set them on the ground. "There's a revolver and ammunition and a whetstone and flour and a pan and a whole lot more."

"All yours," Fargo said.

Petey reached in and pulled out a poke that jingled. He set it on the ground and undid the string and upended it and out clattered coins. "There's pretty near five dollars here."

"All yours," Fargo said again.

Petey replaced the coins. He picked up the Sharps in one hand and the revolver in the other, and giggled. "I can do it. I can honest to God do it."

"Do what?"

"I can—" Petey stopped. He put down the revolver, pressed the rifle's stock to his shoulder, and sighted down the barrel at a tree. "I can be a scout. What else?" He lowered the Sharps. "It's all because of you. My folks would be as grateful as I am. They were everything to me."

The constant praise made Fargo uncomfortable. "Let's see about those buckskins."

It took almost until midnight. Fargo slit the shirt up the side and had Petey slip it on, then trimmed the excess, had Petey remove it, and sat for hours by the fire using a needle and thread. He'd bought them a long time ago to repair his own buckskins but sewing was a trial. He must have stuck himself twenty times before the shirt was done. Then there were the pants.

The belt Kroenig had worn was much too big so Fargo punched extra holes with the tip of his Arkansas toothpick. Petey strapped it on over his buckskin shirt and had to pull practically a third of the belt past the buckle to make it fit. He wrapped the extra around the belt.

"How do I look?"

Green as grass, Fargo thought. Aloud he said, "You've got the makings."

Petey slid the revolver under his belt and hefted the Sharps and grinned at the world and everything in it. "I feel like I could beat anyone."

"Hold on there, sprout," Fargo said. "You have a lot to learn yet before you're ready to tangle with, say, Apaches or Comanches or the Sioux."

"I know that," Petey admitted. "But I don't aim to tangle with them."

"As a scout you go where the army sends you," Fargo enlightened him. "You could end up fighting any or all three."

"He wouldn't let that happen. Not after all He's done to make my wish come true."

"He who?" Fargo said.

"God Almighty."

"Oh hell." Fargo leaned back. "Listen, boy. Believing in the Almighty doesn't make you arrow-proof. A notion like that can get you killed."

"We all have to die sometime," Petey Evans said.

11

The last couple of days Fargo devoted to lessons in shooting the Sharps and the revolver, a Remington, and to having the boy practice his riding.

Petey got so he could draw fairly fast and hit a stump at about five paces but never dead center. As for the Sharps, it kicked like a mule, and after only a few shots Petey complained that his shoulder hurt. He missed more than he hit and was clearly glad when Fargo said they could stop.

Petey had Kroenig's knife, too. Fargo gave him lessons in how to hold it and stab and parry and Petey did the best he could.

"You're better with a blade than you are with guns," Fargo mentioned when they broke to rest. It wasn't saying a whole hell of a lot.

"I'll keep that in mind when I have to kill someone," Petey said.

"I hope you never have to."

"Why do you think I've learned all this?" Petey said. "I want to be as good at it as you are."

That bothered Fargo. It sat in his craw, and on the evening of the last day when they were sitting at the fire, he brought it up by saying, "There's more to life than killing, Petey. I'd hate to think I went to all this effort so you can snuff out a few wicks."

"No, you did it for my forty dollars."

"Don't be cute."

Petey spooned some of the squirrel stew Fargo had cooked into his mouth and hungrily chewed. "I'm sorry if it upsets you. It's not as if I'll make it my life's work or anything." He patted the Remington. "But you have to admit, it's a good feeling to have the power of life and death over somebody."

"I never thought of it that way," Fargo said.

"Then how?"

"I don't think of it at all until my life is threatened and then I get it over with and forget about it."

Petey swallowed and idly tapped his spoon on his bowl. "It's a shame people can't get along, isn't it? If everybody was friendly to everybody else we wouldn't need guns and knives and the like."

"No use wishing for something that will never be," Fargo said.

Petey made as if to say more but gave a toss of his head and resumed eating. When he was done he said, "Will you be heading out tomorrow?"

Fargo nodded. "I hear there's a high-stakes poker game in Saint Louis in a couple of weeks."

"You gamble as well as scout?"

"I do a lot of things," Fargo said. He guided wagon trains, he'd tracked for the Army, and he hunted men on rare occasions.

Petey gazed into the fire and grew sad. "I want to thank you for what you've done."

"Like you said, you paid me forty dollars."

"No. That was wrong of me to say. You did it to help me, I know. It means more than I can put into words."

"Just don't get yourself killed."

The next morning they were up at the crack of dawn. Petey

didn't want breakfast. He saddled the sorrel, shook Fargo's hand and thanked him again, and rode off.

Fargo took his time. He had a long journey ahead of him and would be in the saddle well into the night. He put coffee on and discovered he was almost out. Since the trading post was close by, he decided to stop on his way out of the Musselshell country and buy more.

Tom Carson was behind the bar. Brianna, he said when Fargo asked, wasn't up yet. His manner was gruff, and when Fargo mentioned that he needed coffee, Carson got it and practically slammed it down in front of him.

"What the hell is the matter with you?" Fargo demanded.

"You."

"What did I do?"

"As if you don't know." Carson went down the bar and began arranging bottles.

Fargo followed. "Are you mad about me killing Kroenig?"

Carson paused with a bottle halfway to a shelf. "I didn't even know. When?"

Fargo told him about the shooting and how he gave all of Kroenig's possessions to Petey.

"Good riddance to Kroenig," Carson spat. "He stopped here a lot but he was the kind of customer I could do without."

"Then why are you mad at me?"

"You're worse than Kroenig."

Fargo was growing angry. "I don't beat whores. And I don't try to shoot your other customers."

"No, but you get kids killed," Carson said.

That made no sense to Fargo. "I taught Petey enough that he can be a good scout if he's careful and keeps on learning."

"Is that what he told you? That he wants to be a scout?" Carson uttered a mirthless laugh. "He sure pulled the wool over your eyes."

"You better start explaining."

Carson set down the bottle, and sighed. He selected another, got two glasses, and motioned for Fargo to join him as he went around the bar to a table. Only after he had poured for both of them and taken a sip did he say anything.

"Didn't Petey tell you about his folks?"

"He said they were dead."

"Did he tell you how they died?"

Fargo shook his head.

"Clever of him. He probably figured if you knew, you wouldn't teach him." Carson refilled his glass. "Ever been to the Bitterroots?"

"A few times," Fargo said. The Bitterroot Mountains were part of the Rocky Mountains, and as rugged and remote as any on the continent. They were largely unexplored by whites. The Nez Perce, who were friendly, roamed them. So did the Blackfeet, who weren't friendly to whites the least little bit.

"Settlers have been straying in for a few years now. Word has gotten out that there's plenty of wildlife and water and the land is there for the taking." Carson paused. "Petey's folks aimed to carve out a homestead of their own. They came in a covered wagon with all their possessions."

Fargo grunted. He wasn't particularly fond of settlers. Too many were coming west and turning the wilds into farms and ranches and towns.

"I tried to talk them out of it," Carson said. "I told them the winters are hard as hell but they said they were from Minnesota and they were used to cold weather. I told them the Blackfeet would lift their scalps if they didn't watch out, and they said they didn't aim to let that happen."

"No one does," Fargo said.

"So off they went. Then about two months later Petey showed up alone. He was a mess. Clothes all ripped. So thin he was skin and bones. He asked if I would see fit to sell him a gun on credit. I made him sit down and tell me what happened." Carson drank the rest of his glass in a swallow. "It was the Wolfe gang."

Fargo had heard of them. A gun shark with the handle of Lazarus Wolfe had been terrorizing the northern Rockies for a few years now, murdering homesteaders and attacking wagons, and then disappearing with his gang into the mountain fastness where no one could find them. "The boy never mentioned that."

"Of course not. He didn't want you to know the truth. He didn't have you teach him so he could be a scout. He did it so he could go after Lazarus Wolfe. It's all he's talked about doing since he got here. But he didn't have a gun and he didn't have a horse and he didn't know the first thing about living in the wilds on his own. Now, thanks to you, he does."

"Damn," Fargo said.

"That's right. Right this minute he's on his way to the Bitterroots to get revenge. He doesn't stand a prayer. Lazarus Wolfe will skin him alive." Carson swallowed. "You thought you were doing Petey a favor but all you've really done is gone and gotten him killed."

12

From a distance the Bitterroots were imposing ramparts thrusting skyward to claw at the clouds. There were only a few passes in and out, and Skye Fargo was one of the few white men who knew where each pass was.

He was approaching from the east through the Bitterroot Valley. Watered by the Bitterroot River, it was lush with grass and trees and game. It gave the unwary traveler no inkling that beyond lay perils aplenty.

The Bitterroots were so remote, and so hard to get into, that only a few settlers had ventured there, and for the most part they had settled along its fringes. The Bitterroot Valley was home to several.

Evening was coming on as Fargo neared a large cabin a stone's toss from the river. There was a corral and a barn and a chicken coop. A prosperous homestead, by frontier standards, and the man who owned it had more sense than many. As soon as the family spotted Fargo, the man went inside and came back out with a rifle. His wife appeared, holding one too. Five children, ranging in ages from six or so up to about sixteen, peered through windows or the doorway. Several of the oldest also had long guns.

Fargo drew rein and leaned on his saddle horn and smiled. "I like your army."

"It doesn't pay to be careless," the man said. He was big

44

and brawny and had a face darkened by the sun and seamed by hard work.

"More settlers should be as smart as you," Fargo said.

"What do you want?" the man demanded.

"I'm looking for a boy," Fargo said, "about as old as your boy, there." He nodded at one of the children. "He's riding a sorrel and wears buckskins and carries a Sharps. His name is Petey Evans."

"Nice boy," the man said. "Came through here, what, three days ago?" He glanced at his wife and she nodded. "We let him stay the night and he moved on the next day."

"Three days," Fargo repeated. He'd hoped it was less. Petey was riding hard. Too hard. If the boy wasn't careful, the sorrel would play out and he'd be afoot.

"Are you his pa?" the man asked.

"A friend," Fargo said. He straightened and touched his hat brim to the wife. "Ma'am. Much obliged." He raised his reins to go and the man raised a hand.

"Hold on, mister. You seem decent enough. You're welcome to stay the night if you'd like. There's straw in the barn you can bed down on. And you can join us for supper, too."

The sun was already half gone. Fargo wouldn't get much farther anyway before dark fell. "I reckon that would suit me."

The man lowered his rifle. "I'm Jared Adams. We don't get many visitors out to these parts. It will be nice to have some company."

Fargo well knew how settlers were often starved for news of the rest of the world. They lived so far out that every stranger was an occasion for socializing.

"We eat in half an hour," Adams said. "That'll give you time to strip your animal and wash up." He jerked a thumb at the cabin. "The washbasin is in back."

"Again, I'm obliged," Fargo said.

The barn was cool and shadowed. He put the Ovaro in an empty stall and hung his saddle blanket and saddle over the side.

Someone had filled the washbasin with freshwater and placed lye soap and a towel out. Fargo took off his hat and his red bandanna and scrubbed his face and neck until his skin was raw, then retied the bandanna and swatted the dust from his hat and went around to the front and knocked.

He had been mistaken about the number of kids. There weren't five. There were six. The one who opened the door was the oldest. She had to be close to twenty. With her green eyes and brunette curls and full bosom, she was downright breathtaking.

Fargo felt a twitch below his belt and almost forgot to smile. "How do you do?" he said, extending his hand.

Hers was small and warm and she let it linger. "I'm Myrtle. I saw you through the window."

"Were you hiding?" Fargo joked.

"Yes. Pa doesn't trust strangers until he's talked to them. He says I'm not to show myself until he's sure the stranger is safe."

"Your pa had the right idea."

Myrtle appraised Fargo as someone might appraise a stallion they were about to buy. "Are you safe?"

Fargo looked past her and didn't see anyone. Grinning, he winked and whispered, "No."

"Good," Myrtle said, and stepped aside. "Come on in. Everyone else is at the table."

The cabin smelled of food and tobacco and other pleasant odors. It was well built and comfortable, and Fargo couldn't help thinking what a shame it would be if the Blackfeet paid Adams and his family a visit.

A chair at one end had been saved for him. Fargo pulled it

out and was about to sink down when Mrs. Adams cleared her throat.

"Wouldn't you be more comfortable with your gun belt off?"

"No," Fargo said. He did remove his hat, though, and set it to one side.

"Leave him be, Linda," Jared said. "This one is all right."

"It's not that," Linda said. "It's just not mannerly to wear a gun to table."

"You know, you're right, ma'am," Fargo surprised himself by agreeing. He unbuckled the belt and hung it over the back of the chair so the Colt was in easy reach. A glass of water was next to his plate and he washed the dust of the trail down his throat.

Before him was spread a veritable feast: roast venison cut in thick slabs, potatoes brimming with butter, green beans and peas, biscuits and bread and a small bowl of jam.

Fargo was about to pick up his fork and dig in when he realized the entire family was staring at him as if they were waiting.

"We like to give thanks first," Linda said, clasping her hands and closing her eyes.

Everyone else followed suit.

Fargo clasped his but he didn't close his eyes, and after she had given thanks for the bounty of their meal and their good health and the recent rain for their crops, he unclasped them and said to Jared, "You might not want to do that when you don't know the person."

"Pray?"

"Close your eyes."

Jared Adams blinked. He looked at his wife and his children and said, "My God."

"Jared!" Linda said.

"He's right and I never gave it any thought."

"What is he right about?" Linda asked.

"Closing my eyes when we have a stranger at the table. The stranger could draw a gun and shoot us dead."

Linda looked aghast at Fargo. "How could you think such a thing? How could anyone?"

"The bad ones do."

"We don't invite bad people to eat with us," Linda declared.

"You can't always tell," Fargo said. "Sometimes they hide they are bad until it's too late."

"You're being absurd."

"No, dear, he's not," Jared said.

Linda colored and her jaw muscles twitched.

Fargo hadn't meant to cause a spat. He tried to mend fences by saying, "Your husband doesn't want anything to happen to all of you, ma'am. Out here it's not good to be too trusting."

"What kind of life is that, to never trust anyone? We can't go around thinking everyone is out to do us harm."

"It can't hurt," Fargo said, and grinned.

Linda didn't find it humorous. "The Book says to love thy neighbor."

"Down Texas way they have a saying," Fargo rejoined. "Love your enemies but keep your gun oiled."

"I refuse to mistrust everyone who stops here just because they might do something," she stubbornly insisted.

"Which would you rather be?" Fargo asked. "Trusting and dead or wary and alive?"

Linda Adams had no answer to that.

13

The barn was cozy. A plow horse and a milk cow occupied the other stalls. In a back corner straw bales were stacked. Fargo cut the twine on one and spread straw for his bed.

With his saddle at his back and his blanket pulled to his chest, he was snug and content.

He aimed to get an early start so he'd turned in earlier than he usually would. As full as he was from the meal, he figured he'd drift right off but sleep proved elusive. He tossed. He turned. He got up and went out and around to the back and emptied his bladder. When he came back, Myrtle Adams was sitting where he had been lying. In the dark he could just make out a pink robe that clung enticingly to her curves. Her feet were bare.

"Howdy," she said, and grinned.

"Do your folks know you're here?"

"I snuck out." Myrtle patted the straw next to her. "Have a seat."

Fargo moved to the middle of the aisle and gazed out at the cabin. The windows were all dark.

"What's the matter?" Myrtle asked, and giggled. "Afraid my ma will storm out here with a shotgun?"

"Not your pa?" Fargo said.

"Our ma is the stern one. Sometimes I think she likes taking a switch to our backsides."

"She still takes a switch to you?"

"I'm a grown woman," Myrtle said.

"I noticed."

"Did you?" Myrtle patted the straw again. "Then why are you still standing there?"

Fargo sat so he faced the open barn door. "Are you sure they're asleep?"

"You worry too much." Myrtle leaned toward him. The scent of vanilla wreathed her hair.

"I stay alive longer that way." Fargo admired the swell of her breasts under the robe.

Myrtle leaned closer. "Ma was real mad about what you said at supper. She and Pa had a fight about it."

"Your pa's a good man. I didn't mean to cause him trouble."

"Oh, they squabble a lot anyway. Ma nearly always starts it. Usually at night after we've gone to bed. One thing leads to another and sometimes she yells at him."

"He doesn't yell back?"

"Not Pa. He lets her rant herself out and then he goes to bed."

"Some men wouldn't put up with it," Fargo mentioned.

"Us kids have had to all our lives. But now I'm old enough to strike off on my own."

"Do tell," Fargo said. Her breath was warm on his cheek, her robe a hair's-width from his buckskin shirt.

"It's why I'm here," Myrtle said. "I want you to take me with you."

"Can't."

"Because you're looking for that boy? What was his name? Evans?"

"Because of him," Fargo said.

"Can't he wait?" Myrtle lightly pressed against him. "I want

out of here so much. I'd do anything. Absolutely *anything*."
When he didn't respond she said, "We don't get many visitors. That boy and you are the only two we've had in months. He was too young. But you—" She stopped and touched his cheek. "You're a man and you're handsome as can be."

"I still can't."

Myrtle drew back, her mouth in a pout. "Can't or won't? What's this boy to you, anyhow? Kin of some kind?"

"No."

"Then what?"

Fargo didn't consider it any of her business but he answered, "He's going to get himself killed if I don't stop him from doing something stupid."

Myrtle gave an angry toss of her head. Her brow puckered and she brightened. "Wait a minute. You can do both. Take me with you and we'll hunt for him together."

"He went into the Bitterroots."

"So?"

"So there are hostiles and a mean bastard by the name of Lazarus Wolfe."

"I've heard of him," Myrtle said. "But the Bitterroots go on forever. You could spend a month in there and not come across another living soul."

"True."

"So why not take me? We go in, find the kid, and scoot back out before Wolfe and the Indians have any idea we're there."

"It's too dangerous."

"If I'm willing to chance it, you should be too."

"I'm not you."

Myrtle smiled and pressed against him and placed her hands on his shoulders. "What would it take to persuade you? This?"

She kissed him on the mouth.

Only a fool would have pushed her away and Fargo was no fool. He returned the favor more heatedly than she seemed to expect because when he placed his hands on her breasts she suddenly drew back with a gasp.

"Not so fast."

"I thought it's what you wanted," Fargo said.

"It is, it is," Myrtle assured him. "I just want to be sure we have a deal first."

"Which deal was that?"

Myrtle made no attempt to hide her annoyance. "Damn it, stop playing games. Will you take me or not?"

"Not."

"I am commencing not to like you." Myrtle pushed to her feet and flounced out, her robe tight around her body.

Fargo lay back on his saddle and laced his fingers behind his head. The Ovaro was staring at him, and he chuckled. "That went well," he said.

14

A pink flush suffused the eastern sky when Fargo led the stallion from the barn. He figured to leave before the family was up but most homesteaders weren't lie-abeds. Jared Adams came from the woodshed carrying firewood for the cookstove.

"Morning."

Fargo bobbed his chin.

"You're not lighting a shuck before breakfast I hope. My wife makes the world's best flapjacks."

"I have to catch up to Petey Evans," Fargo said. Now that the Ovaro was rested he could push harder.

"It's not what Linda said, is it?"

"No." Fargo swung up and over and hooked his other boot in the stirrups. He lifted the reins but sat there. "I have to say it. You've been kind to me and I can't let it be." He paused. "You shouldn't be here."

"It's what we want."

"You're too far from anywhere. The Blackfeet find you, you know what will happen."

"Maybe they won't," Jared said. "They haven't so far."

"I wish you luck," Fargo said, and meant it.

"There's something I haven't told you," Jared said. "That boy you're after, Petey Evans? He asked if I'd heard word of Lazarus Wolfe. I told him that last I knew, Wolfe had been seen up around the Lola Trail. That was months ago, though. The boy asked how to find it and I'm afraid I told him."

"It didn't strike you as peculiar, a boy his age wanting to find Lazarus Wolfe?"

"As a matter of fact, it did. I asked what he was up to but he wouldn't say." Jared hefted the firewood. "I hope I haven't gone and gotten him rubbed out."

"I hope so, too," Fargo said, and headed up the valley just as the rooster crowed. The breeze was cool on his face. A pair of ducks winged in and settled on the river. Several doe bounded off with their tails flashing.

"The Lola Trail," Fargo said out loud. It had been used by the Indians since anyone could remember. Lewis and Clark had relied on it to cross the Bitterroots. It was Fargo's understanding that whites named it after a trapper who was killed by a griz years ago. As trails went, it was a bitch. Most of it followed the high ridgelines. Footing for a horse could be treacherous and the wind was a constant nuisance.

The end of the valley came into sight. So did another homestead. This one was smaller but there were as many if not more kids. Fargo didn't count them. He saw a woman in a bonnet at the front window. She smiled. A man came out of a long shed. He smiled, too. No guns anywhere.

"Damn them," Fargo said.

Beyond rose the foothills, stepping-stones into the mountains. A trail wound up from the valley floor. In a patch of bare dirt Fargo spied the sorrel's prints. They were three days old but no one else had been by and it hadn't rained.

Fargo was confident he could overtake the boy. The Ovaro had more stamina than most horses and in the mountains stamina counted for more than speed. Stamina, and surefootedness.

In that respect the Ovaro was a little like a mule. Only a

little, because the reason mules were less prone to slip and fall was due to their shorter, thicker hooves, and slimmer bodies. That, and mules thought for themselves. A horse would nearly always go where the rider wanted. A mule would stop and study things if it didn't like where the rider was going, and if it didn't think it safe, it wouldn't go another step. Fargo had great respect for mules.

He crossed two ridges and drew rein overlooking a narrow valley. Below sat a cabin and an outhouse. A man was chopping a tree and a woman was wringing clothes. Usually he would have given them a wide berth and gone on his own way but he had to know about the boy so he gigged the Ovaro down.

The couple were so intent on their work that he was close enough to pick them off with his Henry when the woman happened to glance up. She gave a start and hollered to the man and he put down his ax and went into the cabin and came back out with a rifle. She stood beside him, the portrait of timidity.

Fargo was fifty feet out when the man shouted that it was close enough. He stopped. By the looks of the cabin and outhouse they were recently built. The couple was young, in their twenties. "Sorry to bother you," he said.

"What do you want?" the man demanded. "We have no food to spare. You want water, there's the stream yonder."

"I'm looking for a boy," Fargo said, and went on to describe Petey Evans.

The man nodded. "We've seen him. Stopped to ask his way to the Lola Trail. Told him I'd never been there but he'd be smart to stay shy of it. We hear that Lazarus Wolfe operates up that way."

"Wolfe operates down this way, too."

"He won't get us like he's done others," the man said with a threatening motion of his rifle at the empty air.

"You wouldn't stand a prayer," Fargo said bluntly.

The man scowled and said over his shoulder, "Don't listen to him, Amanda. He's just trying to scare us."

"Yes," Fargo said. "I am. It's better to be scared and gone than stay and be killed."

"Say no more, mister," the man said angrily. "Here I answer your question and you try to spook us."

"If Lazarus Wolfe finds you, he'll kill you. The same with the Blackfeet."

"I'm not scared of any man, white nor red." The man wagged the rifle. "Be on your way."

Fargo sighed and rode off up the valley to a game trail that took him across a sawtooth ridge. By now he was a good piece into the Bitterroots. Granite peaks towered in massive slabs. Eagles and hawks circled high in the sky. Everywhere there was sign of the multitude of wildlife: grizzlies, black bears, deer, elk, even moose, as well as a host of smaller creatures. Fargo drank it in with the same enthusiasm he drank whiskey. Moments like this, the wilds gave him the same intoxicating feeling.

The next homestead no longer was. Charred ruins of the cabin stood in mute testimony to the stubbornness of human nature, and to its violence. A skeleton lay near the ruins. A jagged cavity in the skull showed where it had been bashed in. Several ribs had been shattered. Around to the side was another skeleton, a female this time, tatters all that was left of her dress.

Fargo climbed down and examined the ground. Faded shod hoofprints revealed that those responsible weren't red. He continued on.

He rode with his senses alert and one hand on the Colt. Danger often struck in the bat of an eye. A man had to be ready. It was either be quick or be dead.

Miles farther he was considerably surprised to find yet another cabin. This one was intact. Smoke curled from the chimney and an old swayback was tied to a peg on the front wall.

Burlap covered the window. He drew rein and cupped a hand to his mouth. "Hello the cabin!"

The door opened and out limped an old man in homespun who spat a wad of tobacco juice and leveled a rifle. "What the hell do you want?"

"Right friendly," Fargo said.

"No, I am not, and I don't care, either. Now what do you want?"

Once again Fargo gave a description of Petey Evans.

"You his pa?"

"No."

"Brother?"

"No?"

"Cousin?"

"No, damn it."

"Friend?"

Fargo shrugged.

"Then what the hell are you looking for him for?"

"He shouldn't be here."

The old-timer nodded. "Agree with you there. Could tell he was green as grass. I offered to let him stay the night but he refused."

"And you as friendly as you are," Fargo said.

"Don't try to get my goat. I don't care for people and I don't pretend I do." The old man gestured at the surrounding peaks. "Why in hell do you think I live so far from everywhere?"

"Because you're such a sociable cuss."

The old man spat more dark juice. "Got that right. Now be on your way."

Fargo went to rein off but stopped. "How is it Lazarus Wolfe hasn't turned you into maggot bait?"

"Maybe he figures I ain't worth the bother."

"Way I hear it, he doesn't care how old they are. Babies, gristle and bone like you, it's all the same to him."

The old man glowered. "Now you're annoying me, mister. Be gone."

"Thanks for the time of day."

Fargo's back prickled as he rode off. He kept his head half turned so he could make sure the old geezer didn't put a slug between his shoulder blades. Something about the old man gnawed at him but he couldn't figure what. Eventually he stopped thinking about it and concentrated on catching up to Petey Evans.

That night he camped on a high shelf in the lea of a rock face that sheltered him from the wind. He made a small fire and had coffee and pemmican and listened to the howls, growls, and shrieks that filled the night. Once something big came close to his fire. He saw its eyes, heard it sniff. A bear, but whether a griz or a black bear he couldn't say. It drifted off, and shortly afterward he lay down and soon was lulled to sleep by the bestial symphony of fang and claw.

15

It was the middle of the next morning when Fargo discovered he was being followed. He'd stopped to give the Ovaro a rest after a steep climb to a lofty bench. He'd dismounted and was arching his back to get rid of a cramp when he gazed down his back trail and spied a rider far in the distance. Just one, but one was enough if it was a backshooter. He watched a while and then climbed on the stallion and rode to a notch in the summit that would take him over this range to the next. The notch was short and wide and flanked by scrub brush. At the other end he drew rein, slid down, and led the Ovaro out of sight. Shucking the Henry from the saddle scabbard, he perched on a boulder and admired the vista of mountains and granite until hooves clinked on rock. He cocked the rifle and stood in shadow. When the rider emerged he stepped into the sunlight with the Henry to his shoulder.

"Small world."

The grizzled old man had his rifle across his saddle and started to jerk it up but thought better of it and froze. "What the hell are you doing?"

"Pointing a gun at you."

"I can see that," the man growled. "What the hell for?"

"I don't like being followed."

"Who's following you, sonny?"

"You are."

The old man's cheeks kept puffing out. "I sure as hell am not."

"Yet here you are," Fargo said. "Why?"

"Why what?"

"Why are you following me?"

"I'm on my way into the high country to hunt elk."

"There are elk all over. You didn't have to come this far."

"I'll hunt where I damn well please. Now I'll thank you to stop pestering me." He raised the reins.

"Drop the rifle."

"Do what now?"

"You heard me."

"I by God will not."

Fargo put his cheek to the Henry and sighted down the barrel. "You by God will."

The old man swore but he gripped his rifle by the muzzle and bent until the stock was a few inches from the ground and let go. "Happy now?"

"What's your handle?"

"Why the hell should I tell you?"

Fargo waited.

"Stricklin. My name is Stricklin."

"Lived in these parts long?"

"What the hell is this? You fixing to rob me or what?"

"Climb down," Fargo said.

"Like hell."

"Do we have to go through this again?" Fargo took aim at Stricklin's shoulder.

"You wouldn't shoot a man who is unarmed."

"Are you sure?"

No, Stricklin wasn't. He cussed fiercely but he swung his leg over the saddle and stood glaring pure spite. "There. Happy now, you bastard?"

"Not yet." Fargo relieved him of a revolver and tossed it into the brush. He picked up the rifle and backed away and tossed it in, too.

"I won't forget this," Stricklin vowed.

Fargo whistled and the Ovaro came over. Without taking his eyes or the Henry off Stricklin, he stepped into the stirrups and gripped the reins. "Don't let me catch you following me again."

"You think you're God Almighty," the old man growled.

"You only get one warning." Fargo wheeled the Ovaro and twisted in the saddle so he could keep Stricklin covered as he started down.

"If there was any law hereabouts I'd have you arrested," Stricklin said.

"Do yourself a favor," Fargo advised. "Whatever you're up to, forget it."

"God Almighty," Stricklin said again.

Fargo went on looking back until he was out of rifle range. The old man stayed where he was. Then Fargo was in timber, and brought the Ovaro to a trot. He descended to a meadow and went around it to the other side. Drawing rein, he climbed down, took the stallion into the pines, and looped the reins around a branch. Then he sat at the meadow's edge with his back to a tree and the Henry in his lap. "It won't be long," he told himself.

It wasn't.

Maybe twenty minutes had gone by when Stricklin materialized at the other end of the meadow. He was hanging from his saddle, reading sign. He had his weapons.

Fargo flattened.

Instead of crossing the meadow, Stricklin rode around it as Fargo had done. Stricklin's bay was almost on top of him when Fargo heaved up out of the tall grass.

"Not again," Stricklin said. He made no move to use his rifle.

"I warned you."

"I'm elk hunting, damn you."

"Get off. Now."

Stricklin stared at the Henry and eased down. He made it a point to hold his rifle out from his side with his hand nowhere near the trigger.

Fargo took the rifle and the revolver and stepped back. His Henry never wavered. "Now you can climb back on."

Stricklin's ratlike eyes narrowed. "Make up your damn mind. Climb down. Climb on. What do you expect me to do next? Ride off and let you keep my hardware?"

"Yes."

Stricklin balled his bony fists. "Mister, I've taken all I'm going to—" His gazed drifted past Fargo and he blanched and said, "Oh, hell."

It was the oldest trick of all and Fargo didn't fall for it. Then a horse nickered off up the mountain and he risked a quick glance.

Indians, a lot of them, were descending toward the meadow—and they were painted for war.

16

In a spurt of speed Fargo was into the trees. Stricklin came after him, tugging on the reins. They stood and watched as the war party came steadily lower.

"Blackfeet," Stricklin whispered as if afraid they could hear him when they were hundreds of yards away yet.

Fargo nodded.

"I count twenty-two of the red buggers."

Fargo had the same tally.

"They don't act as if they saw us," Stricklin said. "But if we stick around they just might." He held out his hand. "I want my guns."

Fargo debated whether to hand them over.

"You can't leave me defenseless," Stricklin urged. "Not if you know how they are. Not if you know what they do to white men."

"I do," Fargo said, and reluctantly did as the man wanted. Stricklin was so relieved he appeared about to cry. He clutched the rifle tight and stared up the mountain. "I haven't seen any of those red devils this far south in a coon's age."

"Could be they're on their way to raid the Nez Perce or the Crows or Shoshones," Fargo speculated.

"Could be," Stricklin agreed. "But it's my hide I'm worried about." He turned and climbed on his horse. "We should get the hell out of here before they spot us."

Fargo moved to the Ovaro. "Stay close." He reined to the north, staying as much as possible in the shadows.

"Thing that worries me," Stricklin said, "is that when there's one bunch, there are sometimes others."

Fargo was acquainted with the Indian practice of splitting war parties into smaller groups so they were less likely to be detected by their enemies. "Keep your eyes skinned."

"Mister, I'm way ahead of you." Stricklin was glancing right and left and over his shoulder.

Fargo skirted a thicket of thorns.

"You know," Stricklin said, "if that boy you're after ran into them, he's dead and gone."

"Maybe he didn't," Fargo said.

"You're one of those glass-half-full folks," Stricklin said. "I hate that. I'm a the-glass-is-empty-and-always-will-be fella."

"I think they call that cynical."

"Then I'm cynical as hell and proud of it." Stricklin glanced over his shoulder and lowered his voice. "But not so cynical I want to lose my hair to prove the world ain't worth a shit."

"Hush," Fargo said.

The war party had reached the meadow. Most of the warriors climbed down to stretched their legs and talk. The majority were armed with bows, more than a few with lances, several with trade rifles. They showed no sign that they thought whites were within a thousand miles.

A clearing opened before them. Fargo went around. Ahead rose a series of slopes to a granite slab so high it seemed to brush the clouds.

"Up there?" Stricklin said. "Why not lie low right here? They can't see us."

"The more distance," Fargo said.

"They have eyes like hawks."

"Better."

"You want to be killed you go right ahead," Stricklin said. "But don't hold it against me if I don't. This is where we part company." He drew rein.

"We shouldn't," Fargo said.

"What are you going to do, shoot me?" Stricklin smirked. "You do and you'll have all those red bucks down on your head."

"It's smarter to stick together."

"Smart for you but not for me." Stricklin spat tobacco juice. "Maybe we'll run into each other again. Maybe sooner than you think."

On that enigmatic note, the old man clucked to his horse and was soon out of sight.

Fargo swallowed his anger. He hadn't learned why Stricklin was following him and now he'd have to watch his back from here on out. Then again, he had to watch it anyway.

He started up the next mountain. He had lost Petey's trail but it was only temporary. Once he shook the war party he'd swing to the west and pick it up again.

Fargo passed a patch of pink flowers. He passed hemlock, wound through a belt of pines. Above grew firs, tall and straight in phalanx ranks, their slender boles purple and blue with shadow. He drew rein and turned.

The war party was just leaving the meadow, heading south.

"Adios," Fargo said, and rode on. He hoped he'd seen the last of them. He had enough to occupy him, what with Petey and Lazarus Wolfe and now Stricklin, and the wild beasts that roamed the Bitterroots.

No sooner did the thought cross his mind than he came out of the firs and there was a bear.

17

Fargo's reaction was to start to draw the Colt but he stopped and did something he rarely did on encountering a bear: he laughed. It wasn't much more than a cub. It took one look at him and made a sound half squeal and half bleat and whirled and raced off. He scoured the vegetation for sign of its mother but if she was close by she didn't appear. Thank God. He rode on unmolested.

Finding Petey's tracks took longer than he expected. The boy was still making for the north into the heart of the Bitterroots.

Fargo camped that night in a hollow high on a windswept spine. Several times he went to the top and gazed out over the benighted terrain. Nowhere was there a glow. If anyone was out there, they were hiding their fire, like he was.

The next day, though, along about eleven in the morning, he spied gray coils rising above the trees. He thought it was a campfire. Cautiously approaching, he drew rein on a timbered spur and stared down at the last thing he expected to find this far in: another cabin. This one was middling size and poorly constructed and there were four horses with saddles tied out front. There was no barn, no outbuildings, no evidence the soil had been tilled for a garden.

"Well now," Fargo said. Climbing down, he settled in to watch a while.

About noon two men came out. They were unkempt and their clothes were rumpled and each was a walking armory. They stood jawing and passing a bottle back and forth. When the bottle was empty one of them threw it away and they each climbed on a horse and rode off together to the north.

Fargo had a hunch what this place was. Only two were left, and since there was no predicting how long they would stay, he forked leather and worked his way down to within hailing distance. But he didn't hail them. He alighted and led the Ovaro, making as little noise as possible.

The door was open. Gruff laughter came from inside, and a gravelly voice.

". . . fought and clawed. I like it when they do that. Gets me fired up."

"I know what you mean," said another man. "The ones that lie there like lumps make me mad."

"Makes you want to beat them," said the gravelly voice.

"Or chuck them off a cliff."

Both men laughed.

Fargo edged to the door. He was careful not to show himself. He heard the clink of a bottle. Then, as best he could, he imitated the sound of a cat.

"Did you hear that?" the gravelly voice said.

"Hear what?"

Fargo did it again.

"That's a damn cat."

"What the hell would a cat be doing way the hell out here? Unless it's a wild one," the other man said. "Maybe it's a bobcat kitten or something."

"Meow," Fargo said, and quickly backed around the corner. Spurs jingled, and shadows splashed the ground.

"Where did it get to?"

Fargo stepped out and said, "Meow."

They were as dirty and their clothes as ill-used as the other pair. Both were looking about for the cat. Both stiffened and one splayed his fingers over his six-shooter but saw that Fargo had his hand on his Colt and didn't draw.

"What the hell?" Gravel Voice said.

"Meow," Fargo said again.

"You must think you're funny, mister."

"Or maybe I like cats." Fargo moved so he had a clear view of both.

"What do you want?" the other demanded. "Who are you, anyhow?"

"Stricklin," Fargo said.

They glanced at one another and the man with the gravel voice said, "I'm starting to get mad. You'd better tell us who you really are and explain yourself, and do it quick."

"I'm with the *Saint Louis Herald*," Fargo said.

"You're what?" Gravel Voice said. "You don't look like no journalist to me. I saw one once and he wore city clothes and a derby."

"I'm doing a story on Lazarus Wolfe and was wondering if either of you is him?"

Their faces hardened and their eyes glittered with craftiness.

"Never heard of him," the other man said.

"Liar," Fargo said.

"I will gun you, by God," Gravel Voice warned.

"Meow," Fargo said.

"You're plumb loco, mister," the other one said. To Gravel Voice he asked, "What do we do with him, Frank?"

"What do you think?" Frank said.

Both went for their revolvers but neither had cleared leather when Fargo's Colt flashed and the hammer clicked. They had the presence of mind to imitate stone.

"Jesus," the other one breathed, his Adam's apple bobbing up and down.

Frank glared. His posture betrayed that he still wanted to draw but he wasn't stupid. He slowly raised his hands out from his sides. "Pretty slick, mister."

"Suppose we have a talk," Fargo said. "Unbuckle your gun belts and let them drop and we'll go inside."

"What if I don't want to?" Frank said.

"I'll shoot you in the leg."

"Do as he says," the other man said.

"I don't like having a pistol pulled on me, Tuttle. I don't like it one little bit."

"Shed," Fargo said.

With baleful resentment, Frank did so. Tuttle was quicker about it, and quicker, too, to back into the cabin when Fargo told them to.

Sunlight streaming in the glassless window did little to relieve the gloom. The place smelled of liquor mixed with the reek of unwashed bodies. A table with cards on it was ringed by five chairs, and a lot of blankets lay to one side in haphazard chaos.

Fargo had them sit and put their hands on the table. He sat where he could see the door and the window and placed the Colt on the table and folded his hands over it. "Isn't this cozy?"

"Know this," Frank said, glowering. "Before this is over I'm going to kill you."

18

Tuttle uttered a nervous chuckle. "Frank doesn't mean that. Tell him you don't mean that, Frank."

"No one pulls a pistol on me."

"Pay him no mind," Tuttle said to Fargo. "What is it you wanted to talk about, mister?"

"The Evanses."

"Who?"

"John and Mary Evans." Fargo recollected Petey telling him their names. "And their son. You haven't happened to have seen him in the past couple of days, have you?"

"I don't know what in hell you're talking about," Frank said.

"We haven't seen no boy," Tuttle declared.

"He was headed this way."

"I tell you we haven't seen him. What's he coming here for?"

"His folks were killed and now he's out to avenge them by killing Lazarus Wolfe."

It was all of ten seconds before Tuttle collected his wits enough to say, "Lazarus who?"

"I never heard of him," Frank said.

Fargo sat back, his hand still on the Colt. "Too bad I won't get to play poker with you two."

"Lazarus who?" Tuttle said again.

"He has a gang," Fargo said. "Frank here, and you, are part of it."

"Like hell," Frank said.

"Are you a lawman?" Tuttle asked. "I don't see no tin star."

"Then I'm probably not."

"Who are you, exactly?" Tuttle pressed. "*What* are you, exactly?"

"I'm pissed off at being lied to."

"That's no answer," Tuttle said.

"How long before Wolfe shows up?" Fargo asked.

Frank was a study in hate. "How many times do we have to tell you, we don't know any Wolfe?"

"I have an idea," Fargo said. "We'll wait for him together. We can play cards and drink and have a grand old time."

"Do you have any idea who Lazarus Wolfe is?" Tuttle said.

"I thought you didn't know him?"

"I've heard of the gent," Tuttle responded. "They say he's as mean as they come. Not normal mean, where a man gets mad and then hits somebody. He's mean all the time. Mean to his core. So mean, he'll shoot you if you look at him wrong."

"You heard all that?"

"You're not taking me serious," Tuttle said.

"How is it you'd ride with a man like that?"

"We don't," Tuttle said. "But if we did, I reckon it would be because we're a little mean, too. And it'd be a heap of fun."

"It's fun to kill and rob and rape?"

Tuttle tried being cagey. He shrugged and said, "There are some as might think so."

"I doubt you do," Fargo said.

71

"Do what?"

"Think."

Frank smacked the table. "Enough of this bullshit. I've had it with your shenanigans. Either shoot us or get your ass out of here."

"Frank," Tuttle said.

"Don't Frank me, you weasel. I don't tuck tail for anyone. Not even when they're holding a gun on me."

"You're awful brave," Fargo said sweetly.

"God, I want to shoot you."

Fargo stood. He deliberately put on a show for them by twirling the Colt forward and in a reverse spin and swirling it into his holster with a flourish, all in the blink of an eye.

"Damn," Tuttle said.

"Lazarus Wolfe can do that," Frank said. "Only a heap faster."

Fargo leaned on the table and smiled. "I thought you didn't know him?"

"I heard he can," Frank amended, and smiled at how clever he was being.

Fargo backed to the door. "When you see this man you've never met, tell him for me that I'm looking for him."

Frank couldn't resist. "I sure as hell will. And then he'll come looking for you and bring the rest of us with him."

"Frank," Tuttle said.

"What?"

Fargo backed out and ran to the Ovaro. He swung up and reined to the east and crossed the clearing to the trees. He didn't think they would wait long and they didn't. Frank stormed out and picked up his gun belt. Tuttle was slower about it and looked all around in fear of being shot.

An argument broke out. Fargo couldn't hear much of what they said, only a few loud words. He gleaned that Frank wanted to come hunting for him but Tuttle was trying to talk him out of it. Eventually Tuttle prevailed. They closed the door and climbed on their horses and headed to the north.

"Worked like a charm," Fargo said to the Ovaro, and grinned.

19

Frank was so mad that he rode glaring straight ahead. Tuttle, the smarter of the pair, nervously looked over his shoulder a lot.

Fargo stayed well back and took advantage of the cover. He'd provoked them to goad them into leading him to Lazarus Wolfe and it appeared to be working. Exactly what he would do when they got to wherever Wolfe was, he hadn't quite figured out.

Frank pushed so hard that Tuttle pleaded with him to ride slower for the sake of their horses.

It was late in the afternoon when two riders appeared in the distance. They were taking their sweet time, and at a holler from Tuttle, they drew rein and waited. It was the pair Fargo had seen leave the cabin earlier.

The four made camp as the sun was setting. Tuttle and one of the other men collected firewood. Frank and the fourth man stayed with the horses. Their meal consisted of jerky and coffee.

Fargo's consisted of a few pieces of pemmican. He didn't dare start a fire of his own unless he went off a ways and he wasn't letting them out of his sight. Hunkered in the dark, he chewed and thought about Petey.

The next morning the four were up and under way at the

blush of daylight. Frank was in the lead, and he was still mad. They stopped at noon. By then they were high on a winding ridge, and on the Lola Trail.

Fargo was glad there had been no trace of the boy.

He wasn't so happy the next morning when they got up and put coffee on and sat around doing nothing. He didn't understand why until a line of riders crested a granite ridge and clattered down the trail and joined them.

Lazarus Wolfe had seven men with him. They were coarse and cold-eyed, cutthroats to the core, the sort of hard cases that law-abiding folks stepped aside for on a city street. Just looking at them you knew they were dangerous. And Lazarus Wolfe was the most dangerous of the bunch. There was something about him, an air of violence, a quality of deadliness possessed by few men Fargo had ever met. Even from a hundred yards away it was as obvious as the sun. When Wolfe moved among them, the others made way. They watched him warily, as a wolf pack might watch its leader. That he was bigger than all of them, even Frank, had more than a little to do with it.

Lazarus Wolfe was seven feet in height if he was an inch and had shoulders as broad as a buckboard. He wore a brown slicker and a brown hat with a short brim and two ivory-handled Smith & Wessons. Two-gun men were rare. Few were really good with one, let alone two. Wolfe always had a big hand on either one or the other.

More coffee was brewed. Lazarus Wolfe and Frank and Tuttle sat and had a long talk, and by Frank's sharp gestures and hard features it was easy for Fargo to guess who they were talking about. Wolfe took turns holding his cup in either his right or his left hand. Frank and Tuttle stopped talking and looked at him expectantly. Wolfe sipped and swallowed and set the cup down and punched Frank in the mouth. It was so quick Fargo almost missed it. He was as surprised as the rest of them.

Frank was the most surprised of all. He recovered, blood running down his chin, and said something. Tuttle tried to put a hand on his arm and Frank swatted it away.

Lazarus Wolfe stood. He took several steps back and lowered his hands to his sides. He said something and Frank started to get up but Tuttle grabbed him. Frank pushed Tuttle down, and rose. The others stepped back to make room. Lazarus Wolfe stared at Frank and Frank stared at him and then Wolfe said a few words and Frank jerked his pistol, or tried to.

Lazarus Wolfe drew, not the right Smith & Wesson or the left one, but both. He drew the twin six-shooters and blasted Frank in the head, and he did it so quickly that if Fargo hadn't been watching, he would have missed it. Then Wolfe did as Fargo had done at the cabin and twirled his pistols, both of them, as fluid and fast as anything, and they were back in their holsters and Frank lay in a heap.

"Damn," Fargo said.

20

Lazarus Wolfe was unusual in being equally expert with a pistol with either hand. He was also unusual in that he was black.

Blacks weren't numerous west of the Mississippi River. Not yet, anyway. Most, in fact, were slaves back east, which was what, in part, the impending war was about.

Eventually, the newspapers claimed, a tide of emigrants would pour west, but for the moment the tide was a trickle, which was why cities and towns were few and far between and why there were so few folks with black skin. Some were townsmen, a few were farmers, and once Fargo had run into a black gambler.

But black gun hands were as rare as hens' teeth, and gun hands of any color as expert as Lazarus Wolfe were even rarer.

It was one of the things Fargo thought about as he sat and watched the outlaws after Wolfe shot Frank. The others seemed to take the killing in stride. Or else they were good at hiding their fear. For it was obvious by how they looked and fidgeted that some of them were very afraid of Lazarus Wolfe. It begged the question Fargo had asked Tuttle: if they were so scared of him, why did they ride with him? The answer wasn't hard to guess. They rode with him because he kept their pokes and their bellies filled. They rode with him because they got to indulge their violent natures. They killed.

They robbed. They raped. To their way of thinking they were in hog heaven.

Fargo considered his plan. So far it had worked. He'd found Lazarus Wolfe. Now he needed to take care of Wolfe before Petey Evans showed up and got himself killed. But take care of Wolfe how? March up to him and challenge him to a gunfight? That was plain stupid. The other outlaws wouldn't sit there and let him gun their leader down. Then there was the important fact that he wasn't sure he could. Lazarus Wolfe was *good*.

How, then, to go about it was the problem Fargo contemplated until the outlaws doused their fire and mounted and headed back the way Frank and Tuttle had come. They passed within a hundred feet of Fargo's hiding place.

He took his time going after them. He wouldn't lose them.

As he rode he worried about Petey Evans. It was good the boy hadn't shown up, and yet there should have been sign of him by now. He wondered if Petey had gotten lost. Greenhorns did that a lot. And a lot of them perished of hunger and thirst. Or were caught by hostiles. Or were torn apart by wild beasts.

Fargo put Petey from his mind for the time being. He focused on the tracks and on the wilds around him.

The outlaws rode until well after dark and then made camp.

They kindled a large fire and sat around it drinking and talking and joking.

Fargo took a risk. He tied the Ovaro, crept to within fifty feet, and sank onto his belly. As silently as an Apache he crawled close enough to the circle of firelight to hear what they were saying. He was interested in learning more about Lazarus Wolfe.

Wolfe had a silver flask and was taking occasional sips. He didn't talk much. For the most part he morosely stared into the flames. He had a broad face and a large nose that had a slight crook in it. He also had a large scar on his left cheek. He was ugly and yet he was handsome. He also radiated a sense of power like the sun gave off light and heat. He made Fargo think of a keg of black powder ready to explode at the slightest spark.

The others left him to his dark musings.

Then Wolfe capped the flask and stuck it in an inside pocket of his slicker and sat up. "Tell me about him again," he said. He had a deep voice, rich in timbre, the kind that drew attention to itself. He was looking at Tuttle.

Tuttle didn't like being looked at. He squirmed and said almost meekly, "Frank and me said all there was."

"Frank is dead," Wolfe reminded him.

Tuttle swallowed.

"Tell me again," Wolfe said.

"Well, he's big. Not as big as you but he's bigger than most. Wears buckskins. Claimed he was with a newspaper when any jackass could tell he wasn't. And he's slick with his six-shooter. Mighty damn slick."

"Quick as me?"

Tuttle laughed, and so did some of the others. "No one is as quick as you."

"He say why he was looking for me?"

"No." Tuttle shook his head. "He did ask about a family called Evans, I think it was. Said as how we'd killed them. And there was something about a boy."

"Could he be kin of theirs?"

"He didn't say he was."

"Tell me again about the cat part."

Tuttled shifted and swallowed. "Well, he pretended to be a cat to draw us outside. Kept saying 'meow' until Frank wanted to shoot him."

"Frank should have," Lazarus Wolfe said.

"He got the drop on us, remember?"

"No excuse."

"But—" Tuttle began, and abruptly stopped. He went pale, and the men nearest to him moved slightly away.

"But what?" Wolfe said.

"Nothing."

"Finish," Wolfe said.

"I'd rather not."

Lazarus Wolfe's voice became a silken growl. "When I tell you to do something, you damn well better do it."

"I just—" Tuttle stopped again, and took a deep breath. "Frank was my pard. I didn't think it fair of you to gun him like that."

"I left him in charge down there."

"I know."

"And what have I told all of you to do when strangers come nosing around?"

"We're to put windows in their skulls."

"And did he? Did you?"

"I told you. We couldn't. He had us covered."

"There were two of you and only one of him."

"But he'd have shot one or both of us before we got him."

"And?" Wolfe said.

"Frank and me would have been dead."

"You say that as if you think it matters."

Tuttle wouldn't look Wolfe in the eyes. To the ground he said, "We ride with you. Shouldn't it matter just a little bit?"

Lazarus Wolfe laughed. The sort of laugh a grizzly would make if grizzlies could laugh. "What do you think, boys? Did Tuttle miss his calling? He should have been a parson."

A lot of them laughed.

"Here now," Tuttle meekly whined.

"Let me make it plain," Lazarus Wolfe said. "The only one that matters to me is me. You want to ride with me, you do as I say. And don't ever give me guff. Frank didn't kill the stranger like he should have, and then he went and gave me guff about it."

"What are we going to do about the stranger, anyhow?" another outlaw asked.

"What do you think?" Lazarus Wolfe said. "We're going to hunt him down. I'll ask him a few questions and if I don't like his answers, I'll kill him."

"I can't wait for that," Tuttle said.

21

Fargo got another surprise when the outlaws reached their cabin. A large party of Blackfeet was camped right beside it. The same bunch as before, if his guess was right, the warriors and many of their horses painted for war. Yet they didn't attack the outlaws. To the contrary. Lazarus Wolfe dismounted and walked over to them and a tall warrior rose and greeted him warmly. A pipe was produced, and Lazarus sat and smoked with their leaders. They used sign language, and since Fargo was as versed in it as any white man alive, he learned why the Blackfeet and the outlaws were on such good terms: Lazarus Wolfe was supplying the Blackfeet with guns.

The chief was there to find out when Wolfe would have more.

Wolfe signed that it would be within two moons, or two months. The chief signed that he needed them sooner as he wanted to make war on the Crows. Wolfe replied that he would try.

At one point the chief called Wolfe his "brother in blood." At another the chief signed that they had a trait in common: they both hated the white man. Wolfe stared at his own men over by the cabin and nodded.

The parley ended and the Blackfeet went off to the west.

Wolfe and his men stripped their horses and Wolfe and half a dozen others went in the cabin. The rest settled outside.

Hunkered in the forest, Fargo mulled what to do. He'd learned a lot but what good did it do him? How was he to deal with Lazarus Wolfe? He could, he supposed, pick him off from hiding with the Henry. But it went against his grain. He wasn't an assassin. As much as Wolfe deserved killing, he wouldn't do it in a cowardly fashion.

An idea came to him, an idea so bold, so brazen, it sent a tingle through him. It could easily get him killed yet the spice of danger made it that much more appealing. He mulled it over until he fell asleep about midnight. He mulled it when he woke up shortly before dawn, and came to a decision.

Fargo sat and ate pemmican and watched the eastern sky gradually brighten. A blaze of color painted the horizon, and then the sun was up and the outlaws who had slept outside stirred. He waited until he saw Tuttle sit up, and then he climbed on the Ovaro and rode out of the woods.

Tuttle was yawning. His hat had come off and he jammed it on and scratched himself and did more yawning. He started to stretch and saw Fargo and froze with his mouth agape. Scrambling to his feet, he ran to the cabin, flung the door wide, and flew inside.

Fargo drew rein, his right hand close to his holster. Other outlaws were looking at him in puzzlement and curiosity. They were too befuddled by sleep to figure out who he was. "Nice day if it doesn't rain," he remarked.

Tuttle scurried back out. Behind him came others, hastily strapping on gun belts and blinking sleep from their eyes.

Last to emerge was Lazarus Wolfe. Icy arrogance marked his scarred face. He wasn't wearing his slicker or hat. On either hip gleamed his ivory-handled Smith & Wessons. "You've got balls, mister."

"And glad I do," Fargo said.

Wolfe cocked his head. "How's that again?"

"As much as I like the ladies, it would be a shame if I didn't."

Apparently this wasn't what Lazarus Wolfe expected. "I hear you've been looking for me."

"That I have," Fargo admitted. "But that lunkhead"—he nodded at Tuttle—"and his friend wouldn't take me to you so I waited around for you to show up."

Tuttle and some others had their hands on their six-shooters but Fargo wasn't worried they'd pull on him. They wouldn't do a thing unless Wolfe said to.

"You don't say," Lazarus replied. "And you went to all this bother why?"

"I'm surprised you can't guess," Fargo said. "I want to join up with your bunch."

"What?" Tuttle bleated, and received a sharp glance from Wolfe.

"Why should I believe you?" Wolfe said.

"Why shouldn't you?" Fargo rejoined. "Who else would go to so much trouble to track you down?"

"A lawman," Wolfe said.

"Do you see a tin star?"

"Doesn't mean you're not. But we'll let that be for now. Tell me why I should let you."

"A man like you can always use a good gun at his side," Fargo said.

"Are you good?"

"Some folks think so."

"How about we find out?" Wolfe said. He glanced at a scruffy man. "Clymore?"

"Yes, boss?"

"You're almost as fast as me."

"Thanks, boss."

"Shoot this son of a bitch."

22

Clymore didn't hesitate. He flashed his hand to his revolver and jerked it.

Fargo didn't hesitate, either. He drew and fired before Clymore could level his weapon, fired again as Clymore staggered and struggled to shoot, fired a third time and the tip of Clymore's nose dissolved and Clymore keeled to the ground and was still.

The rest of the outlaws were rooted in place.

"Hell in a basket," one blurted.

"Did you see that?"

"I told you he was fast," Tuttle said. "I told you none of us can hold a candle to him."

"Except me," Lazarus Wolfe said.

"Except you," Tuttle hastily agreed.

Fargo reloaded. No one tried to stop him. He finished and twirled the Colt into his holster. "Do I get to ride with you or not?"

"We'll see," Lazarus Wolfe said. "We'll talk some, first. Tuttle, you take care of the body. Strip everything we can use before you drag it into the trees and leave it for the coyotes."

"Why me?" Tuttle said.

"Because I said to. Bring me any money he has." Wolfe turned and went in.

Fargo swung down and followed. "You trust Tuttle not to keep some of the money for himself?"

Lazarus Wolfe didn't respond right away. He went over to the bunkbeds and took his slicker from the top one and shrugged into it and his hat from a bedpost and put it on. Sauntering to the table, he pulled out a chair with his foot and sat, his boots propped on the table. "Have a seat."

Fargo chose a chair where he could see Wolfe and the doorway, both.

"I don't trust anyone," Lazarus Wolfe finally answered. "But I do trust in fear."

"Fear?" Fargo repeated.

"The fear of dying. Every white nigger out there knows I'll shoot him dead if he so much as looks at me crosswise. Tuttle keep some of the money?" Wolfe snorted. "I say 'boo' and he wets his pants. He won't keep a cent."

"You're awful confident."

Wolfe shrugged. "A man doesn't believe in himself, what good is he?" He gazed out the doorway. "They'd turn on me in a minute if they thought they could get away with it. Fear keeps them in line."

"There are safer ways to make a living," Fargo said.

"But not any I'd like." Wolfe laughed. "I get to kill white people anytime I want."

"Indians too."

"No," Wolfe said. "I don't ever kill Indians unless they make me." He paused. "Whites, now. That's another story. I hate them so much, I'd kill every one there is if I could."

"You ride with whites."

"I have to ride with somebody. I can't do it all myself. It's poetic, me riding with men who like to kill their own kind as much as I do."

"Poetic?"

Wolfe's good humor evaporated. "I can't know words like that because I'm black?"

"I didn't say that."

"You didn't have to," Wolfe said. "But then, you're white too, and all whites think all blacks are as dumb as tree stumps."

"Not all whites," Fargo said.

Lazarus Wolfe was quiet a bit. "You ever been a slave, mister?"

Fargo shook his head. It was a silly question.

"My pa was, and his pa before him. I was born into slavery, and I hated it from the day I was old enough to understand what it was. I was born a darkie in a world run by whites. Growing up, all I heard was, 'Lazarus do this' and 'Lazarus do that.' And do you know what the overseer did if little Lazarus didn't do it good enough to suit him?"

Fargo didn't say anything. He had a feeling Wolfe didn't really want him to.

"I got beat with a switch. When I was older I was whipped. I still got the scars." Wolfe squirmed in his chair as if his back itched. "By the time I was ten I made up my mind. I wasn't going to be a slave my whole life like my pa and his pa. I was going to be free. So guess what I did?"

Fargo stayed silent.

"One night when I was fourteen, I snuck out of the shack the seven of us lived in. It wasn't no bigger than an outhouse, but that's not important. What counts is I snuck over to the overseer's and bashed his brains out with a hammer I'd stole. Hit him so many times, his head was mush."

Fargo saw it in his mind's eye.

"And do you know what?" Wolfe smiled. "I'd never been so happy in my life as I was standing over him and seeing all that blood and bits of him all over his pillow. I would have gone on to the mansion and killed the plantation owner but he had dogs he kept chained close. And besides, I wanted my freedom more. So I stole a horse and headed west and here I am."

"All the robbing and killing you do," Fargo said, "you're getting back at whites for what they did to you."

"Smart boy," Lazarus Wolfe said mockingly, and suddenly grew somber. "Now let's talk about you. How come you want to join up with me?"

"I'm on the run from the law," Fargo fibbed.

Wolfe nodded at the door. "So's every one of those bastards out yonder."

"You and your men are the talk of the territory." Fargo piled it on. "To tell the truth, I'm tired of being on my own."

"Tired of looking over your shoulder, huh? I can savvy that. I'm not saying I believe you, mind. I'll think on it some."

"You think I'm lying?"

"I read people real good," Wolfe said. "I can't read a book but I can people. Take Tuttle. Yellow through and through. Gets his courage from a bottle or from being around men who have it. Clymore? Fancied himself a gun hand. Might have tried me one day but now he never will."

"That's why you picked him to draw on me?"

"Two birds," Wolfe said. "I wanted to find out if you were as good as Tuttle and Frank claimed, and if you were, I got rid of a nuisance."

"Smart boy," Fargo said.

Lazarus Wolfe's featured hardened. "You get to call me that once. But only once. It's what they called me on the plantation. They never used my name. It was always *boy*. Boy this and boy that. Got so, I hated the word as much as I hated being a slave. You ever call me it again, I'll gun you."

"You'll try," Fargo said.

Wolfe smirked. "I like a man with confidence. You're a

little like me, I think. You don't take any guff. And you've got balls."

"But?" Fargo said.

"But there's something about you I don't quite trust. Can't say what it is yet. If you want to ride with us while I figure it out, you can."

"What happens then?"

"I'll either let you join us permanent," Lazarus Wolfe said, "or we'll see which of us is slowest." And he pointed a finger at Fargo and let down his thumb as if it were a revolver hammer.

23

The rest of the outlaws didn't trust Fargo any more than their leader. He saw it in their eyes. He noticed how some of them put their hands on their six-shooters whenever his hand was near his holster.

That evening Fargo joined the gang around a fire as they ate their supper. A man called Tatum was their cook, and was terrible at it. He'd made squirrel stew but he'd only been able to shoot one squirrel and then added a few wild onions and a little flour. Calling it stew was wishful thinking. Soup was more like it, and watery soup, at that. Most of the outlaws drank it as they would coffee.

Fargo had had worse meals but he couldn't remember when. Every now and then there was a morsel to chew on, and he was nibbling at a tidbit of meat when Lazarus Wolfe got up and walked around the fire to Tatum and flung his stew in Tatum's face.

Everyone else stopped eating and talking.

Tatum recoiled in fear and wiped a sleeve across his eyes. "Is something the matter?"

"I'm sick of the slop you feed us."

"I do the best I can."

"It ain't good enough."

Tatum showed some gumption. "Don't blame me. You picked me to do this, remember? All because I'd worked in a restaurant once. I told you that all I did was clean tables, that you'd be better off having someone else fix your grub. But you wouldn't listen."

Wolfe placed his hands on his Smith & Wessons. "I'm listening now."

"It's just not fair," Tatum said. "Maybe I could do a little better if I had more to cook with. I can't help it I'm not much of a hunter."

"Neither is anyone else," Tuttle remarked.

Fargo sat up. He'd had a brainstorm, a way he could win them over and also have some time to himself.

"I can hunt," he said.

All of them looked at him.

"I'm a damn good hunter," Fargo boasted, but it was true. "Squirrel, rabbit, deer, you name it, I can keep the supper pot filled."

"Bold talk," Tuttle said.

"It'd be good to have meat regular, though," another outlaw said.

"God, what I'd do for a steak," said a third. "Mostly we eat like birds."

"It's not my fault," Tatum protested.

Lazarus Wolfe took his hands off his revolvers. "We'll find out. Starting tomorrow, Fargo, here, does our hunting. Tatum, you only have to do the cooking."

"What if he doesn't bring me anything?" Tatum asked.

Wolfe looked straight at Fargo. "Then I'll have to teach him not to brag unless he can back it up."

"You'll see," Fargo said.

"We better."

Wolfe sat back down and the talking and drinking resumed. They were each allowed a few swallows from a bottle, but no more.

When it came to Fargo's turn, he drank and smacked his lips and said, "I could use a whole bottle."

"Couldn't we all?" an outlaw by the name of Briscoll said. "But we only have a couple left and they have to last."

"For how long?" Fargo asked.

"That's the hell of it," Briscoll said. "We never know."

"Sometimes we hit a cabin or some wagons and we get lucky," Tuttle said. "Other times they're teetotalers. Damn them to hell."

Fargo learned a lot more before the outlaws turned in for the night. Not only were they nearly always short of food and whiskey—they were nearly always on the go. Wolfe never stayed anywhere for more than a few days, even their cabin. They constantly prowled the Bitterroots for people to prey on. It was a hard, grueling life, yet they stuck with it.

Fargo slept with his blanket pulled to his chest and his Colt in his hand. He was uneasy being among so many killers.

The slightest sound woke him. Toward dawn he slept for an hour but it wasn't near enough. He was worn and tired when a golden crown blazed the eastern sky. He got up and kindled the fire and put coffee on.

The outlaws went on sleeping.

All save one.

Spurs jingled, and out of the cabin strode Lazarus Wolfe, fully dressed. He squatted and held his hands to the flames to warm them. "You're like me. Always up at the crack of day."

"Habit," Fargo said.

An outlaw snored loud enough to shake the cabin, and Wolfe glanced at his men in disgust. "Look at them. It'll be noon before they're all up. Some I'll have to kick out of their blankets."

"You don't like them much, do you?"

"I don't like them at all." Wolfe rubbed his hands together. "Do you know why they live like they do? On the wrong side of the law?"

"They like the killing and the robbing," Fargo said.

"There's that," Wolfe agreed. "But mainly they do it because they're so goddamn lazy. They'd rather live like animals than do real work."

Fargo was going to point out that Wolfe lived the same as they did when the undergrowth across the clearing parted and a face peered out at them.

The face of Petey Evans.

24

Fargo was grateful for the many hours he'd spent at poker. Lazarus Wolfe was looking at him when he spied Petey but he didn't let on.

"They're next to worthless but I need them," Lazarus Wolfe was saying. "I can't do this alone."

"What is it you're trying to do besides kill whites?" Fargo said. Over across the clearing, Petey retreated into the greenery.

"That's enough."

Fargo tried to imagine a hate so strong, so potent, it was all a person lived for. "You never hanker for a wife? Or for a home?"

"What the hell kind of talk is that from a man like you?"

Fargo shrugged. "It's what most men want out of life."

"We're not most men."

"No," Fargo agreed. "We're not." He stood and stretched and said, "If all goes well I'll be back by noon."

"Where do you think you're going?"

"To hunt, remember? I've seen plenty of deer sign. Or are you partial to more squirrel stew?"

"I hate squirrel." Wolfe let out a sigh. "Sometimes I miss what I ate growing up. I'd kill for some corn pone and turnip greens."

"Not much I can do about that," Fargo said. "Venison will have to do." He collected his saddle and saddle blanket and bridle and went about getting ready. All the while he watched the woods for more sign of Petey. He wouldn't put it past the boy to take a shot at Wolfe and bring the whole gang down on his head. As he was tightening the cinch he thought he saw movement but he couldn't be sure. Once astride the Ovaro, he made for the spot.

An outlaw sat up and saw him and started to say something but noticed Wolfe by the fire and lay back down.

The woods closed around him. Fargo went another ten yards and drew rein. "Pete?" he whispered.

"Here," came a reply from farther in.

Not that long ago a giant spruce had uprooted. The branches still had needles on them. It was perfect cover for Petey Evans and the sorrel. The boy was gaunt from not eating enough but otherwise he appeared fine.

"So you found them," Fargo said as he came to a stop.

"And you," Petey said, and raised the Sharps to his shoulder.

"What the hell are you doing?"

"All that talk about being a scout." Petey thumbed the hammer back. "And all the time you were one of them. You ride with the Wolfe gang."

"Like hell I do, you idiot," Fargo said.

"I saw you with my own eyes," Petey said. "Over there talking to him. Just the two of you, as pleasant as you please." He sighted down the barrel. "I don't remember you being with them when they killed my folks but that don't matter. You're one of them and I aim to do to you what I'm fixing to do to the rest."

Fargo's tempered flared. He reminded himself what the boy had been through, and explained, "I came here looking for you and joined up with them."

"Likely story."

"Tom Carson told me about your folks. You lied to me

about wanting to be a scout. The whole time, you were out for revenge."

Petey lowered the rifle to his chest. "I almost believe you. You sure didn't strike me as no outlaw."

"You go against them, you don't stand a prayer."

"Is that why you came? To try and stop me?"

"I didn't teach you what I know so you can go and get yourself killed."

Petey carefully let down the Sharps' hammer and set the stock on the ground. "It was my ma and pa those butchers killed."

"That's still no excuse."

"They were my *parents*," Petey declared much too loudly. "I had to stand and watch."

"Quiet down," Fargo cautioned.

"Nothing you say, nothing you do, will stop me," Petey vowed.

Fargo debated what to do. His impulse was to knock the boy over the head, throw him over the sorrel, and get the hell out of there. But then what? He couldn't keep Petey with him forever, and as soon as he cut the boy loose, Petey would come looking for Wolfe again. "How about if we go off and talk about it?"

"I'm not going anywhere. I've finally found them and before this day is done, I'm putting a bullet in Lazarus Wolfe's noggin."

"Damn it. You *are* an idiot."

"Quit calling me that."

"Yell, why don't you?" Fargo said. "Bring all of them down on us."

Petey turned and walked off, thumping the ground with the Sharps. He came to an oak and placed a hand on the bole and bowed his head.

"Hell," Fargo said. He climbed down and went over. "If you want to be treated like a man, you have to act like one."

"Let me ask you something," Petey said.

"I'm waiting," Fargo said when the boy didn't go on.

"What would you do if someone killed people you cared for? Be honest with me."

"I'd shoot the sons of bitches."

"Then why do you object to me doing the same?" Petey looked up. A tear was trickling down his cheek. "I loved my folks. They loved me. I can't let Wolfe and his men get away with what they did. I just can't."

"But—" Fargo began, and stopped. The boy was right. He couldn't fault him for doing what he would do.

"I'm asking you straight out," Petey said. "Will you help me or not?"

"You could get killed."

"If I let that stop me, it's the same as tucking tail." Petey gripped Fargo's arm. "I'll ask you again. *Will you help me?*"

Fargo had come this far, he couldn't bring himself to back out now. "On one condition."

"Name it."

"We do this my way."

"Your way, my way," Petey said, and shrugged. "Just so Lazarus Wolfe gets dead."

25

The deer tracks led through pines and deciduous trees. Fargo rode with the Henry across his saddle, a round already in the chamber. Chipmunks scampered from his path. A jay screeched off in the trees. Once a raven flew over, the rhythmic swish of its flapping wings beating loud in the rarefied air.

Fargo saw other animal sign besides the deer. He came across elk tracks but the elk were long gone. Bear prints warned of a bruin in the area. The mud along a small stream provided a treasure trove of spoor: fox, wolves, bobcat. All had been there to quench their thirst. So had the prey they fed on.

At that time of the morning deer liked to lie up in cover and rest. Those Fargo was following were no exception. Their tracks pointed into a thicket that covered more than an acre. Dismounting, he wrapped the reins around a limb. On foot he moved along the edge and peered into the tangled depths. It appeared to be a solid mass of vegetation but looks were often deceiving. Game trails led into its very heart.

Crouched low, Fargo glided forward. He placed each foot carefully. He must be quiet. Deer had sharp ears and would bound off at the first hint of danger.

The trail wound like a snake. Fargo avoided branches that might snag his buckskins. He had gone a good distance when a flicker of movement caused him to freeze. He focused on the spot. The movement was repeated. Peering intently, he made out an ear and then the whole head of a doe lying on the ground. Near her were several others. He inched forward. Beyond was a clear space, and the deer. They hadn't spotted him. Slowly, he raised the Henry. He lined up the front sight and the back sight and took a deep breath to steady his aim.

One of the deer saw him and snorted and sprang erect. The rest immediately did the same.

Fargo kept the sights steady. The doe he had chosen was starting to flee when he stroked the trigger. At the blast she staggered. Her front legs buckled and she pitched over and thrashed. The other deer never looked back. Tails high, they fled in bounding leaps.

Fargo worked the lever but another shot wasn't needed. He had a choice. He could skin and butcher the doe there and wrap the meat in her hide or he could take her back and do it at the cabin. He decided to take her back. Petey was the reason. He didn't entirely trust the boy to do as he wanted.

The sun was about at its zenith when Fargo came out of the forest. The outlaws were up. Most were around a fire, drinking coffee and talking. He drew rein and hoisted the doe over his shoulder. She was heavy and had the smell all deer had.

"I'll be damned," Tuttle said. "You did it."

"At last we'll have some meat," Briscoll said.

"Maybe then you'll stop bitching about my cooking," Tatum told him.

They suddenly fell silent. Lazarus Wolfe had come out of the cabin. His thumbs hooked in his gun belt, he moved like a well-muscled panther. "So you *can* hunt," he said.

Fargo squatted and was about to draw his Arkansas toothpick from its ankle sheath, but he didn't. It wouldn't have been smart to let them know he had it. "I lost my knife a while ago. Any chance someone would lend me one?"

Briscoll reached behind him and held out a bowie. "Use mine. I can't wait to bite into a thick steak."

Fargo tested the blade with his thumb. It was honed to razor-sharpness. He inserted the tip and sliced, aware that Wolfe was staring at him. "Something on your mind?"

"You see any sign of anyone when you were off hunting?"

Fargo kept cutting. "No. Why do you ask?"

"I forgot to tell you there are Blackfeet hereabouts. They know my men and leave them be but they don't know about you."

"I'm one of you now?"

"Didn't say that," Wolfe replied. "Just don't want you dead until I make up my mind."

"That's comforting," Fargo said. He had made a slit up the doe's belly. Now he commenced to cut slits up the legs so the hide would peel easier.

"If you have to be killed, I want to do it myself," Wolfe said.

"Didn't realize you cared," Fargo said while slicing.

"I don't," Wolfe said flatly. "But some of my men think maybe you're as fast as me. If I decide you're to die, I aim to show them they're wrong."

"Thanks for the warning."

Wolfe started to turn. "I don't like being prodded. I don't like it even a little bit. Something you should keep in mind." He went back into the cabin.

Briscoll came closer and watched Fargo work. "You take chances, mister. Talking to Wolfe like that can get you dead. He wasn't kidding about the prodding."

"I doubt he kids about much at all."

Briscoll thought about that and said, "You're right. I hardly ever see him laugh. He takes everything serious. Especially killing."

"So do I," Skye Fargo said.

26

The sun was perched on the rim of the earth. Vivid pink and orange painted the western sky. Around the fire, the outlaws gorged and drank and were having a merry time.

The fattest of them patted his belly and said, "That's the most I've ate in weeks."

"Damn, that was good," another said.

Briscoll raised the bottle that was being passed around and said, "Let's drink to the hunter."

"How about drinking to me?" Tatum said. "I cooked the damn thing."

"It's real hard to roast meat on a spit," Tuttle said. "Glad you didn't burn it."

"You go to hell," Tatum said.

Fargo was done eating and sat back with his arm propped behind him. Soon the sun would go down. That was when Petey was to sneak in close.

Lazarus Wolfe sat slightly apart from the rest, sipping coffee. He hardly ever spoke but he did now. "So if I was to take a vote, you boys would vote to let our hunter stay?"

"I sure would," Briscoll said. "Eating regular beats being half starved."

"Me too," another chimed in. "There have been spells when we've gone without for two or three days."

"I do what I can," Tatum said.

"This ain't about your cooking, you jackass," Tuttle said. "It's about having food to cook."

"Call me that again and see what happens."

"Tatum," Wolfe said quietly.

Tatum stiffened and shriveled and held out both hands. "I didn't mean nothing. I get tired of the bellyaching, is all."

"I'd stop talking, were I you," Wolfe said.

Tatum did.

Fargo was watching the woods to the west, hoping Petey would wait as he was supposed to. Consequently he was one of the last to spy the rider who came into the clearing from the south, leading another animal, until one of them pointed.

"Look who it is."

"And look what he's got with him!"

Excited murmurs broke out.

Fargo felt his gut ball into a knot. This was the last thing he expected. Anything could happen. He rose and casually placed his hand on his Colt.

The rider was Stricklin. The old man had his rifle in the crook of an arm and was tugging on a lead rope.

On the horse behind him, slumped in despair, her wrists bound and her moth gagged, was Myrtle Adams. She saw the outlaws and her body became rigid with fear.

Lazarus Wolfe put down his tin cup and moved past the others. "What have we here?" he said as the old man came to a stop.

"I've brought you a present," Stricklin said, and spat tobacco juice.

"Have you been keeping an eye out for new settlers for us to pay a visit?" Wolfe said.

"I'm here with her, ain't I?" Stricklin answered, with a bob of his head at Myrtle Adams.

"That's not what I asked."

"Sure I have," Stricklin quickly said. "I always do as you tell me, don't I?" He tiredly slid down and put a hand to the small of his back and grimaced. "Been riding all damn day. Doesn't do my old bones good."

"You let me know the day your old bones can't take it anymore," Wolfe said, "and I'll get someone to take your place."

Stricklin stopped grimacing. "Damn it, what's the matter with you? I come all the way up here with her and you treat me like this?"

"You're supposed to let me know about everyone who comes up the trail from the south," Wolfe said.

"And I do."

"Oh?" Wolfe shifted and pointed at Fargo. "What about him?"

Stricklin reacted as if he had been jabbed with a sharp stick. "Oh, hell."

"I'm waiting," Wolfe said.

The other outlaws fell silent. A few appeared eager for blood to be spilled.

"He didn't slip by me. Honest," Stricklin said. "And if you don't believe, ask him."

Wolfe looked at Fargo.

"I stopped at his cabin," Fargo admitted.

"And?" Wolfe prompted.

"He dogged me a ways so I took his rifle. I hadn't made up my mind what to do with him when we ran into a Blackfoot war party."

"And?" Wolfe prompted again.

"He went one way and I went another," Fargo said.

Wolfe faced Stricklin. "Took your rifle?"

"He got the drop on me."

"Twice," Fargo said.

"Well now," Wolfe said.

Stricklin glared at Fargo. "You're trying to get me in trouble, you son of a bitch."

"You *are* in trouble," Lazarus Wolfe said. "You don't do as I tell you, what use are you to me?"

The old man licked his thin lips and looked at the other outlaws as if hoping one of them would speak in his defense. No one did.

"Maybe I should have someone else watch the south trail," Wolfe said. Without taking his eyes off of Stricklin, he turned his head and said, "How about you, Briscoll? You interested?"

Briscoll laughed. "In sleeping warm and cozy in a cabin instead of on the ground? You bet."

"There you go," Wolfe said.

"This ain't right," Stricklin said, panic in his tone. "I caught this girl, didn't I? And wait until you hear what she told me." He glanced at Fargo.

"Twice," Wolfe said.

Stricklin took a step back. "Now you just hold on, damn you."

"Are you telling me what to do?"

"You know I never would." Stricklin was pasty white and his right eye was twitching.

"You're holding a rifle. Try to use it if you want. Not that it will do you any good."

"What's gotten in you, you stupid nig—"

Just like that, the Smith & Wessons were in Lazarus Wolfe's hands and he shot Stricklin in the mouth. Both slugs tore through the old man's skull and ruptured out the back of his head in an explosion of hair and bone and bits of brain. Stricklin's horse whinnied and reared, its front hooves flailing, and Wolfe shot it in the head, the two shots booming as one. The horse crashed to the ground and kicked a few times and went limp.

"Son of a bitch!" Briscoll exclaimed, and laughed.

Some of the others laughed, too, nervous laughter fraught with the fear that it could well have been any of them instead of Stricklin.

"I never did like him," Tuttle said.

Lazarus Wolfe twirled his pistols into their holsters. "Somebody drag this old buzzard off."

"I will," Fargo volunteered.

"Make sure you take him far enough that the rot won't bother us." Wolfe turned to Myrtle Adams. "What do we have here?" He stepped to her horse and put his hand on her leg.

"At least Stricklin did one thing right." He looked at his men and winked. "He brought us dessert."

27

Fargo had a reason for wanting to haul the body off. He grabbed hold of both ankles and dragged it. No one paid attention. They were only interested in Myrtle.

Fargo figured she was safe for the time being. The outlaws, like cats with a mouse, would play with her before it turned ugly.

The woods closed around him. Fargo went a dozen steps and stopped. "Petey?" he whispered. The boy was supposed to be there but he got no answer. "Petey?" he whispered again.

"What was it you just said?"

Fargo spun. In his concern for the boy he hadn't realized that Briscoll had followed him. "What do you want?"

"Thought you could use a hand." Briscoll bent and gripped the old man's wrists. "We've got to take him farther than this or Wolfe will be mad."

Fargo was at a loss as to where Petey had gotten to. It didn't bode well.

"Wasn't that something, Wolfe blowing Stricklin's brains out?" Briscoll said between puffs.

"It was a sight," Fargo agreed.

"That's Wolfe for you. You never know but when he'll gun one of us down."

"Yet you stay with him."

"Believe it or not, I've ridden with worse."

They skirted a pine. Fargo ducked under a low limb and almost lost his hat.

"Did you see that girl?"

"Couldn't miss her," Fargo said. In a way it was good that the outlaw was so gabby. It would drown out any noise Petey made.

"She's pretty as a peach," Briscoll declared. "I tell you, I can't hardly wait for my turn tonight."

"All of you will have her?"

"That's how we do it." Briscoll grunted with the effort of dragging so much deadweight.

"Wolfe never keeps a woman for himself?"

"Hell, I suspect he doesn't even like them. In all the time I've been with him, I've never once seen him bed a female. The rest of us ain't as fussy."

Fargo was looking for Petey without being obvious. He didn't see the boy anywhere. Finally he stopped and straightened. "This should do."

Briscoll nodded and let go. "Stupid Stricklin never did know when to keep his mouth shut."

As Fargo went around the body, Briscoll clapped him on the back.

"You sure came along at the right time. I was so sick of eating Tatum's slop, I wanted to pound him with a rock."

"The next time I go out I'll go after elk," Fargo said to make small talk. He was still looking for Petey.

"My mouth is watering already," Briscoll said. "The meat I like best is buffalo but there ain't a lot of the critters in these parts."

"Cougar meat is good," Fargo absently remarked.

Briscoll scrunched up his face. "Eat mountain lion? Are you loco?"

"The old trappers used to like it."

"Sounds like something they would do. They were half strange. Froze their asses off in cold water, always had hostiles breathing down their necks, and all the rest they put up with. And for what? A few beaver hides."

"There are a lot of strange people around."

"Don't I know it. I'm just glad I ain't one of them."

Myrtle was off the horse and by the fire, her legs curled under her. She was still bound and gagged, her eyes mirrors of pure terror as the outlaws laughed and poked her and made remarks about her body and what they would like to do to her.

Lazarus Wolfe was studying her as if making up his mind about something. He looked up when Fargo and Briscoll rejoined them. "Did you take him far enough that we won't smell the stink?"

"We did," Briscoll said.

"You better have." Wolfe turned to Fargo and motioned at Myrtle. "What do you think of our little beauty?"

"She's right fine." Fargo was trying to catch her gaze so he could warn her not to say she knew him but she stared in stark fear at everyone except him.

"I suppose," Wolfe said.

Tuttle smacked his lips as if he were sucking on hard molasses. "When do we get her?"

"When I say so." Wolfe grabbed Myrtle by the arm. She tried to pull away and he cuffed her across the cheek hard enough that her head rocked. "Don't give me trouble, bitch." Myrtle burst into tears.

"I hate when a woman cries," Wolfe said. He drew his knife and cut the rope around her wrists, then pulled on the dirty cloth that had been stuffed into her mouth.

Myrtle commenced spitting and coughing. She recoiled when Wolfe gripped her wrist and received another hard cuff. "Stop that!" she wailed.

Wolfe hit her and she cried out and fell back, dazed. "Don't talk unless I say you can."

"You don't—" Myrtle sputtered.

Wolfed kicked her in the ribs.

A keening shriek of pain tore from Myrtle's throat.

Fargo wrapped his fingers around the Colt. He was ready to intervene if need be. Fortunately, the girl had the presence of mind not to say anything more. She lay gasping and sobbing, an arm over her face.

"That's better," Wolfe said. "You have a minute to catch your breath. Then you're going to answer some questions."

An outlaw reached out to touch her but drew his arm back at a snarl from Wolfe.

"Did I say you could yet? No one lays a hand on her until we find out who she is and what she's doing in these mountains by her lonesome."

"We still get to have her tonight, don't we?" Tuttle eagerly asked.

"Once I'm done with her," Lazarus Wolfe said, "you can rape her to your heart's content."

28

Fargo had to stand there and do nothing as Lazarus Wolfe practically threw Myrtle into the cabin. He didn't dare try to free her, surrounded as he was by the outlaws. No one followed Wolfe in. Girding himself, he did what none of the others were brave enough to.

Wolfe shoved Myrtle into a chair. Somehow he sensed someone was behind him and whirled with his hands on his revolvers. "What the hell do you want?"

"I've seen her before," Fargo said. "She lives in a cabin in the Bitterroot Valley. I stopped there for a meal and spent the night."

"You don't say." Wolfe gripped Myrtle's chin and squeezed. "Is that the truth?"

"Yes, Wolfe, yes!" Myrtle mewed. "We didn't know he was one of your men."

"He wasn't then," Wolfe said, letting go. "How is it you know who I am?"

"That wicked old man told me," Myrtle answered. "I'd heard of you, of course. You're famous in these parts."

Was it Fargo's imagination or did Lazarus Wolfe puff out his chest a smidgen and square his wide shoulders?

"What did you hear, girl?"

Myrtle hesitated. "What everyone does."

"Don't make me beat it out of you."

In a rush Myrtle said, "I've heard that you're a murderer. That you rob people and have your way with women."

"Anything else?"

"That anyone you get your hands on isn't ever seen again." Myrtle was quaking. "That you're as bad as they come."

"I'm worse."

Once again Fargo tried to catch Myrtle's eye but she wouldn't take hers off of Wolfe.

"You do any of that to me and you'll regret it," she blustered. "The army will come after you."

Fargo thought that Wolfe would hit her again but instead Wolfe laughed.

"Hell, girl. Nobody comes this far in. Why do you think I've lasted so long? There's no law except these." Wolfe patted his revolvers, then pulled out a chair across from her and sat. "Let's get to it. Why were you in these mountains alone?"

Myrtle finally looked at Fargo. He touched his chest and shook his head, once, quickly, praying she would catch on.

"I asked you a damn question."

"Sorry," Myrtle said. "I'm so scared, is all. I can hardly think straight." She took a deep breath. "I ran away from home."

"Why?"

"I was tired of my ma and pa always telling me what I could and couldn't do. I was tired of living so far from anywhere. I was tired of having to cook and sew. I was tired of having my brothers and sisters underfoot all the time."

"Is that all?" Wolfe mocked her.

"I want a new life," Myrtle said. She looked at Fargo again. "I thought maybe I'd find a man willing to take me to San Francisco or some such place, where the ladies wear fancy dresses and have servants to wait on them hand and foot."

Fargo had it, then. She'd followed him, hoping she could

get him to change his mind. Instead, she had blundered onto Sticklin, and now here she was.

"Stupid," Wolfe said.

"What's wrong with that?" Myrtle asked. "Everyone should have a dream, shouldn't they?"

"Your kind is never happy with what you've got. You always have to have more."

"My *kind*?" Myrtle said.

"Women."

"I take it you don't like females much."

"There is no use for them that I can see," Lazarus Wolfe told her.

"We have the babies."

"Ain't saying much, to bring a newborn into this world." Wolfe folded his arms. "I reckon I'll let you sit in here a spell and rest. After supper the fun will begin."

"Please," Myrtle said. She reached across and placed her hand on his arm. "Don't let them hurt me. I'll do anything, anything at all."

"Take your hand off me."

"I mean it. Give me a chance. Let me stay in here with you. I'll cook. Mend your clothes. Whatever you want. Even *that* if need be."

Wolfe abruptly stood and glared at her. "Not one more word or I'll gun you where you sit." Wheeling, he strode past Fargo, saying, "I need some air. Keep an eye on her."

Fargo nodded, and the moment they were alone, he stepped to the table. "You damned idiot. Look at the mess you're in."

Myrtle clutched his sleeve. "You have to help me. You have to get me out of this."

First Petey Evans, now her. Fargo swore.

"Why are you so mad? I haven't done anything."

"Except maybe got us killed."

29

Myrtle Adams burst into tears. Hysterics was more like it. She wailed and screeched, her hands over her face, bending to the table and rising up, over and over. It was the crying fit of a child in a woman's body.

Fargo went and leaned against the doorjamb. Lazarus Wolfe had gone a short way and was pacing back and forth with his hands clasped behind his back. The other outlaws were at the fire finishing their meals and nursing a bottle.

Fargo scanned the forest. Still no sign of Petey Evans.

He didn't know what to think. The boy had promised to do as he wanted and now had disappeared.

The wailing went on and on. Some of the outlaws glanced at the cabin in annoyance. Apparently they liked those they were about to rape to be calm about it.

Fargo had to get the girl out of there, find Petey, and skedaddle. A tall order, given that he was one man against many, and hundreds of miles from civilization.

Wolfe stopped pacing and stood gazing into the distance, deep in thought.

Myrtle had run out of emotional steam and was sobbing and sniffling.

Fargo went to the table. "Listen," he whispered, "our best bet is to wait until they're asleep and then we can sneak off."

Myrtle nodded. "Thank you," she said, and swiped her face with her sleeve.

Fargo knew she didn't fully comprehend. "They won't fall asleep until after they're done with you."

Her head snapped up. Her face was still wet and her nose needed wiping. "What are you saying? We can't go until *after*?"

"Keep your voice down."

"You can't let them. You have to protect me. Any decent man would die rather than let a lady be dishonored."

"You young fool," Fargo said.

"*Please*," she beseeched him, and grabbed his arm. "It would be vile beyond words. I don't know as I could stand it."

"If I try to take you out now, we won't reach the horses," Fargo said. Not with that many guns against them.

Myrtle set to wailing anew.

Fargo was turning toward the door when a shot boomed. Just one, a blast of thunder made by a heavy-caliber rifle. Two swift pistol shots followed it. He raced outside to find the outlaws leaping to their feet and drawing revolvers and grabbing rifles.

Their leader held a smoking pistol in each big hand. He was facing the woods, and he gestured and said, "It came from in there."

The rest of them plunged into the vegetation but Fargo stopped and said, "What happened?"

"Someone took a shot at me." Wolfe holstered his right Smith & Wesson and touched a tear in his slicker. "Damn near drew blood, too." His eyes narrowed. "Why aren't you with the girl like I told you?"

"Thought you might need help," Fargo said, and turned to go back.

"Wait. You're our best tracker. Get out there with the others and find the bastard. I'll watch her."

"You sure?" Fargo said without thinking.

"I'm always sure," Wolfe growled. "Do what the hell I tell you."

Fargo ran into the woods. Now that he thought about it, this had worked out in his favor. Wolfe wouldn't touch Myrtle. He could concentrate on finding Petey. It had to be the boy who shot at Wolfe.

The outlaws had spread out and the undergrowth crackled and snapped to their passage. They weren't trying to be stealthy. They were checking behind every tree and log and poking into every thicket.

Fargo caught up to them and slowed. Ahead, an outlaw whose name he didn't know was peering under a pine. Fargo glanced both ways. No one else was near. He holstered the Colt. Stooping, he hiked his pants and palmed the Arkansas toothpick. He held it behind his leg and was almost to the outlaw when the man gave a slight start and turned.

"Oh. It's you."

"Wolfe sent me to help."

"No sign of the bushwhacker yet," the outlaw said, his dark eyes darting right and left. "But whoever it was couldn't have gotten far."

"Let's keep searching," Fargo said, and when the man turned, he stepped in close, clamped a hand over his mouth, and thrust the toothpick into the base of his skull. The man stiffened. He cried out but Fargo's fingers muffled most of the cry. He tore at Fargo's hand and went to reach behind him, and collapsed.

Fargo lowered the body and rolled it under the pine. He was tempted to take the man's pistol but the others might notice and wonder how he had come by it. He wiped the tooth-pick on the man's shirt and hurried on. Soon he saw another outlaw, a heavyset cutthroat with a scraggily beard. "Any sign of who took the shot?"

The man shook his head. "We thought we heard someone run off."

Fargo checked that none of the others were in sight.

"Was Wolfe hit?" the man asked.

"Nicked," Fargo said.

"It must be a damned redskin."

"I thought Wolfe was on good terms with them," Fargo mentioned, his right hand at his knee.

"You can't ever trust those red vermin," the outlaw said. "Wolfe might but I sure as hell don't."

Fargo nodded as if he agreed with the man's sentiments. The outlaw pivoted, and Fargo lunged and sheared the tooth-pick into the man's thick neck, slicing the jugular. Blood gushed as the man squawked and let his rifle fall and grabbed his neck.

He looked at Fargo in astonishment even as his knees buckled and he sank in slow motion to the ground. He didn't shout or scream. He just died.

Fargo cleaned the blade on the man's vest and pushed the body into high weeds. The outlaws were still making a lot of noise. He spotted another one.

It was Tuttle, and he was a bundle of raw nerves. "What are you doing here? I thought you were watching the girl."

"Wolfe told me to lend a hand," Fargo said. "Seen anything?"

Tuttle shook his head. His revolver was cocked, his finger curled around the trigger. "Not yet. You ask me, we should have stayed at the cabin. There might be more than one."

Fargo had the toothpick behind his hip, ready to strike.

But Tuttle kept glancing at him. "Someone said they think it might be Indians."

"Could be. Could be a white man, too. Doesn't much matter. Anyone takes a shot at us, they're goners. It's another of Wolfe's rules."

"He has a rule about that?"

Tuttle nodded. "He says we don't ever leave an enemy alive." Tuttle motioned. "Move off a ways. We're not supposed to bunch together."

Fargo made as if to go, intending to attack the instant Tuttle turned his head, when there were two shots off to the left, and loud shouts.

"They must have got him!" Tuttle exclaimed. He dashed off to see.

Petey, Fargo thought, and after quickly sliding the Arkansas toothpick into his ankle sheath, he broke into a sprint.

30

But it wasn't the boy; it was the boy's horse. Half a dozen outlaws ringed it when Fargo got there. An outlaw with a shotgun had hold of the reins and was acting as if he'd found a rich vein of gold.

"He can't get away now!" the man crowed. "We have him, thanks to me."

"Cranden, you jackass," another said.

"You're giving him more time to escape."

"He can't, I tell you," Cranden said. "Not without his horse."

Briscoll was the last to arrive. He looked around and said, "Where's Turner and Adler? I don't see them anywhere."

"They must still be searching," Tuttle said.

"That's what we better get to doing or Wolfe will have our hides."

"I'll take this sorrel back," Cranden said.

Fargo was scouring the brush. Petey had to be around there somewhere. The boy wouldn't run off without his mount. He turned to trail after the others and caught movement in a tree.

A branch midway up a spruce moved and a pair of eyes peered down at him. He bent and fiddled with a spur. One by one the outlaws vanished into the vegetation, and he was alone.

Putting a finger to his lips, he beckoned.

Petey came down the tree with the agility of a monkey. He was smiling. Before Fargo could stop him, he blurted, "I shot him! I shot Lazarus Wolfe!"

Fargo put a hand over the boy's mouth before he could say anything else. No one appeared to have heard. "Keep your voice down."

"Sorry," Petey whispered when Fargo removed his hand. "I almost made it to my horse when I heard them coming so I hid in the tree. Pretty smart, huh?"

"Pretty dumb," Fargo said. "And you only nicked Wolfe."

Petey forgot himself. "No!" he said, and then whispered, "I was so sure. I did everything just like you taught me. Held my breath. Didn't jerk the trigger. Everything."

"You were supposed to wait. We were to do it together."

"I couldn't," Petey said. "I'm sorry. But the more I thought about it, the more it ate at me."

"We have to get you and the girl out," Fargo said, and headed for the cabin.

"Myrtle Adams? I saw that old man bring her. I stayed with her family one night. She's real nice."

"She's dumb like you."

"I wish you'd stop calling me that."

"You didn't listen to me. You missed Wolfe. You've lost your horse. You've let the outlaws know you're here and they're after you. If that's not a whole lot of stupid, I don't know what is."

"You sure can be mean."

"Boy," Fargo said. "You haven't seen anything yet." He moved faster and Petey matched his stride. "I hope you had the brains to reload the Sharps."

Petey's embarrassed look was answer enough. "I still have my pistol," he said petulantly.

"Quiet."

Fargo had made up his mind. There would never be a better time. Only Wolfe and Cranden would be there. He jogged until the cabin came into sight, then crouched and drew the Colt.

Wolfe was listening to Cranden tell about discovering the sorrel. Wolfe motioned, and Cranden led it around to the side of the cabin.

Petey was taking a cartridge from his pouch. "There he is! This time I won't miss."

"This time you won't try," Fargo said.

"Why not?"

"I'll do it."

"He didn't kill your folks. He killed mine."

"I'll shoot him and get the girl," Fargo proposed. "You fetch my horse and yours and one for her. We'll run off the rest."

About to insert the cartridge, Petey said, "Do you think you can? Shoot a man in the back, I mean."

"Who said anything about doing it in the back?"

"I hear he's terribly fast. You must be sure you can beat him."

"He is fast." And no, Fargo wasn't sure. Lazarus Wolfe had some of the quickest hands he'd ever seen.

"And you call me stupid?" Petey whispered. "The smart thing is to shoot him from ambush."

"It would be safest," Fargo conceded.

"Then why, for God's sake? What are you trying to prove?"

Fargo didn't answer.

"Don't tell me, then," Petey said. He raised the Sharps. "And don't expect me to be like you. From the front, in the back, I'll kill him any way I can."

Wolfe had gone back in. Cranden was coming around to the front.

"Stay put until I'm inside," Fargo instructed, and rose. He holstered the Colt and strolled across the clearing whistling to himself. Inwardly, he was a churning cauldron of uncertainty.

Suddenly Cranden was in the doorway. "Oh. It's you. I wondered who it was."

"I need to talk to Wolfe," Fargo said.

From inside came a curt, "Who's out there? That sounds like our hunter."

"It is," Cranden said over his shoulder.

"I told him to help find who shot me. What the hell is he doing here?"

"Did you hear him?" Cranden asked.

"Yes," Fargo said.

"Then why aren't you out in the woods with everybody else?"

"I have things to do."

"What kind of things?"

With the swiftness of a striking rattler, Fargo drew and jammed the muzzle against Cranden's chest. Bleating in surprise, Cranden clawed for his six-gun. Fargo fired. He tried to push Cranden aside but Cranden keeled against the jamb, blocking the doorway. Fargo pushed harder. Gurgling deep in his throat, Cranden tottered. Fargo shot him a second time, and as Cranden folded, he sprang inside. He had the Colt up and out but he didn't shoot.

Myrtle was on her feet. Behind her, holding a cocked Smith & Wesson to her temple, was Lazarus Wolfe.

"Drop it."

"No." Fargo was well aware that the outlaws in the woods had heard the shots and would hurry back.

"You don't, I'll shoot her."

"Shoot then."

Lazarus Wolfe seemed as taken aback as Myrtle. "You don't care?"

"She's nothing to me," Fargo said. He had the Colt trained on Wolfe's face but if he fired, Wolfe's trigger finger might twitch.

Myrtle was terrified. "Don't shoot, don't shoot, don't shoot," she squealed.

"Shut up," Wolfe said.

"Let her go," Fargo said. "You do, and I give you my word I won't start it."

"I should have shot you when you came through the door instead of grabbing her."

"That's what I would have done."

"I don't make mistakes often."

"You made one now." Fargo heard whinnies and a commotion from the side of the cabin.

"I can drop you before you shoot."

"Maybe you can. Maybe you can't." Fargo smiled. "And if I tie you, you're dead."

"Damn me," Wolfe said.

From off in the woods came yells.

"My men will be here soon."

"It'll take them a couple of minutes yet," Fargo said. "I'll be gone by then or one or both of us will be dead."

"Your word?" Wolfe said.

"I gave it."

Lazarus Wolfe nodded. "This ain't the way. When we do it, we should do it right."

Fargo nodded.

Wolfe pointed the Smith & Wesson at the ceiling and took a step back. "The bitch is yours."

"What's going on?" Myrtle said.

"Get moving," Wolfe said, and pushed her.

Myrtle stumbled and caught hold of the table to keep from falling. She was utterly confused and looked at Wolfe and then at Fargo. "What do I do?"

Fargo beckoned. "Hurry." He kept the Colt on Wolfe and gestured for her to go out the door. Petey had brought the horses up. Fargo started to back out.

"We're coming after you," Wolfe said.

"I wouldn't expect different."

"When I catch you, we'll settle this. Just you and me. You have *my* word on that."

"Something to look forward to," Skye Fargo said.

31

They rode as if the hounds of Hell were on their heels. And the hounds of Hell were.

Neither Petey nor Myrtle rode well. Petey had a habit of flapping his arms and legs while Myrtle clung to the mane of her animal in fear of falling off.

Fargo was heading for the Bitterroot Valley. Their only hope was to get out of the mountains. Maybe, just maybe, Wolfe wouldn't leave his sanctuary.

They rode all the rest of that day, stopping to rest their animals as often as they had to. Myrtle chafed with impatience each time. She was anxious to escape.

Petey wasn't. Their third rest, he paced and looked back the way they had come and said, "I don't see any sign of them."

"You sound as if you want to," Fargo said.

"I do. Lazarus Wolfe is still alive."

"You don't know when you're well off. Be thankful you're still breathing."

"Don't give me that," Petey said. "You keep forgetting what they did. I won't. Not as long as I live. I won't put it to rest until each and every one of them is dead."

"I thought it was Wolfe you were after."

"For starters," Petey said. "He's their leader."

"I'll say one thing for you," Fargo said by way of praise. "You don't think small."

Myrtle had been sitting with her head bowed but now she looked up. "I may not get the chance later on, and I want to thank you for saving me."

"Your folks are probably worried sick," Fargo mentioned.

"I know. It can't be helped. I couldn't live there anymore. I felt so"—Myrtle paused, her brow creased—"so stifled."

"I don't blame you."

"You don't?"

Fargo encompassed the mountains with a sweep of his arm. "I like the wilds as much as anyone. But I also like a card game and a dove and a bottle of whiskey. Civilization has its uses."

"It has plenty," Myrtle agreed. "Fine clothes. Fine food. Most of all, it has the one thing life out here doesn't."

"And what would that be?"

"A good night's sleep."

Petey scratched his head. "I don't follow you."

"Out here a day doesn't go by that I don't worry about hostiles paying us a visit, or outlaws, or that a grizzly will come out of the woods and tear one of us apart," Myrtle related. "It wakes me up at night. I'll lie in bed in a cold sweat and just hate it."

"Oh," Petey said.

Fargo saw the boy blush at the mention of her lying in bed, and chuckled.

"East of the Mississippi there are no such worries," Myrtle continued. "No hostiles. Few outlaws. No grizzlies or hungry wolves or buffalo that can gore you and trample you to death. People go their whole lives through without having to worry about any of that. They sleep peacefully at night. I want that. I want to never have to worry."

"Good luck with that," Fargo said.

Petey cleared his throat. "After I'm done getting revenge

for my folks, I can do whatever I please. And I was thinking that maybe I'd head back east, myself."

"What about being a scout?" Fargo asked.

"I misled you. I admit it." Petey hadn't taken his eyes off of Myrtle. "So I was wondering, Miss Adams. Maybe you and me could go back together. That way I could look after you, sort of."

"How old are you?" Myrtle asked.

Petey did more blushing. "Fourteen."

"I'm five years older than you."

"So?" Petey said.

Myrtle shrugged. "I don't know. I'll think about it. You are big for your age, and you're awful brave."

Fargo thought the boy's head would explode, his face got so red.

"Thank you, ma'am."

"Don't call me that. It makes me sound old."

"Miss Adams, then."

"No. We're friends. You can call me by my first name."

"I'd be happy to," Petey said, sounding as if she had just bestowed knighthood on him.

Fargo turned to the Ovaro. "Enough chatter. It's hours until sundown. We can put a lot of miles behind us."

"Do you think they'll catch us?" Myrtle asked. "And be honest with me."

"I'd be surprised if they didn't," Fargo admitted.

On they went, until the sun was an orange Cyclops on the western horizon and the shadows had lengthened to monstrous proportions.

On a windswept ridge that afforded a mile-long view of their back trail, Fargo made camp. He got a small fire going where it was sheltered by a boulder. They sat eager for the coffee to get done and nibbled on pemmican from his saddlebags.

Myrtle and Petey were quiet. They sat across from each other, and every now and then Petey would glance at her adoringly.

The howl of a wolf heralded the advent of night. It was the cue for a chorus of cries and screams and roars from all quarters. Once a bear chuffed near them and Myrtle stiffened and half rose as if to bolt.

"Sit back down," Fargo said. The last thing he needed was her blundering around in the dark.

"Didn't you hear that? It's a grizzly and it's close."

"Usually they leave people be."

"Not always," Myrtle said fearfully.

Fargo knew that better than anyone but to put her at ease he said, "Usually a griz will show itself first. It will sniff to get our scent and make up its mind whether it wants to eat us or not."

"You say that so calmly. Doesn't it scare you, being eaten by a bear?"

"I'm not going to piss my pants over something that might not happen." Fargo stood and moved around the boulder and stared out over the veil of ink to the north. "Hell."

"What is it?"

Myrtle and Petey joined him. Both saw the dot of light in the distance.

"It's them, isn't it?"

"None other," Fargo confirmed. Indians wouldn't make a fire that could be seen from that far off.

Petey Evans rubbed his hands with glee. "Good. I can't wait to kill some of them."

"Provided they don't kill you first," Fargo said.

32

More hard riding, from daybreak until noon. Fargo drew rein on the crest of a granite spine. Forested slopes spliced by winding valleys stretched for as far as his hawk's eyes could see.

"Any sign of them?" Myrtle anxiously asked.

"Not yet, but they're back there somewhere." Fargo dismounted. "Ten minutes and we head out."

"I feel like I've been riding forever," Myrtle complained. "My legs are so sore I can barely stand."

"Then sit," Fargo said.

Petey waited for her to pick a spot and then sat near her, the Sharps across his legs. "I can't wait until they come into rifle range." He patted the Sharps. "They're in for a surprise."

"You might be too," Fargo said.

"How so?"

"They'll be shooting back."

Petey sniffed and said, "I'm not worried. Besides, you told me a Sharps can shoot farther than most rifles."

"If the person knows how to shoot it."

"You taught me, remember?" Petey said smugly.

"Not good enough or you wouldn't have missed Lazarus Wolfe."

"I'll do it right next time. Wait and see."

"Quit your squabbling," Myrtle said irritably. "So what if

you can shoot? There are a lot more of them than there are of us."

"We'll pick them off one at a time," Petey said.

"And what will they be doing? Cowering in fear? I think not." Myrtle was in a mood. "Skye is right but you're too stubborn to see it. We are in deep trouble."

"I'm not stubborn," Petey said.

Fargo walked a few yards and turned in a complete circle. He saw a bald eagle soaring to the southwest. He saw light brown specks that could have been mountain sheep to the west. A grosbeak was warbling to the east. Then he turned to the south and every sinew in his body tightened. "Just what we needed."

Myrtle heard him. "What is it now?"

"See for yourself?" Fargo said, and pointed.

A mile or more away, a line of riders filed along a switch-back. They were too distant to tell a lot about them but one aspect was apparent: all wore buckskins.

"Are those Indians?" Myrtle asked, aghast.

"A Blackfoot war party," Fargo said.

"They're coming this way," Petey noted.

"My God," Myrtle said. "We'll be caught between them and the outlaws."

"I'll protect you," Petey said.

"How? Let them fill you with their arrows and when they don't have any more to shoot, I can ride off?"

"Why are you being so mean to me?" Petey asked.

"Stop being foolish and I won't."

"The two of you could drive a man to drink," Fargo said. He gazed to the north. Riders were crossing a high summit about the same distance away as the Indians.

The other two saw them, too.

"That's Lazarus Wolfe," Myrtle said.

"You have good eyes," Fargo said.

"What do we do? We can't just sit here and wait for the redskins and those badmen to reach us."

Petey coughed to get their attention. "If we shoot Wolfe and the Indian leading that war party the rest will turn tail."

"Or try harder to kill us," Fargo said. He wasn't letting on but he was considerably worried. Wolfe and company were bad enough. If the Blackfeet got wind of them, they would be lucky to escape with their hair. "We need to light a shuck."

Fargo climbed on the Ovaro. With the outlaws to the north and the war party to the south, they had two options. West would take them deeper into the Bitterroots. East would take them out of the mountains, and later they could bear to the south to reach Bitterroot Valley. So east it was.

The afternoon crawled toward evening. When they came to meadows or other clear spots Fargo twisted in the saddle. Just as the sun was going down he was rewarded with the sight of riders moving along a crest from the north. That would be Lazarus Wolfe. Not a minute later another line of riders was silhouetted coming from the south. That would be the war party. They met in the middle and halted.

Myrtle was looking back. "What do we do if they join forces?"

"Ride faster," Fargo said.

Petey laughed. "We don't have anything to worry about. We're too far ahead."

"You don't know anything," Myrtle said.

Fargo shared her sentiment. Youth and inexperience killed more people than smallpox.

Night fell. The sky was moonless, a lot of the starlight blocked by clouds.

Fargo stopped in a clearing in a stand of fir trees. He went through the ritual of making coffee and handing out pemmican.

"It will be nice to eat a real meal again," Myrtle commented as she gloomily munched.

Fargo had a lot to say so he got to it. "Listen carefully. Unless we slow them we're done for. Neither of you would be any good at it so that leaves me. In the morning you two go on ahead. I'll stay and do what I can."

"Just us alone?" Myrtle shook her head. "Not on your life. We'd get lost or starve."

"I can tell direction," Petey said. "Fargo taught me."

"Then you go on if you want but I'm staying with him," Myrtle said.

Both Fargo and Petey said at the same time, "No."

"I'll do what I please, thank you very much. And I please to stay with Skye. Nothing you say or do will change my mind."

"You don't care about staying alive?" Fargo said.

"When that vile old man got hold of me and dragged me off to Lazarus Wolfe, I was scared out of my wits. I was all alone and sure I was going to die. It taught me a lesson." Myrtle smiled fiercely. "If I do have to go, I'd like it to be with a friend at my side."

"You've always got me," Petey said.

33

Fargo had a plan. He announced that they would make camp where they were, and he set off to hunt while Petey and Myrtle stripped the horses and gathered firewood. He didn't have to go far when he flushed a grouse. The big bird took wing and he brought it down with a snap shot from the Henry. He carried the bird back and dropped it beside Myrtle, who was resting with her chin on her knees.

"What am I supposed to do with this?"

"Pluck it."

"I hate doing that. My mother always made me pluck the chickens and I got feathers in my hair and up my nose."

"I'll do it for her," Petey offered.

"Thank you." Myrtle smiled sweetly.

Fargo almost said no, that she had to do it, but if she got mad at him it would make his plan harder to carry out so he let it go. He used his foot to roll the grouse over to Petey. "Do a good job."

"One thing I am good at is plucking birds," Petey said. "I used to do it on the farm and I did it a lot for Mr. Carson."

Fargo faced to the west. Tonight there was no telltale glow to tell him where his enemies were. He wondered if they had decided not to stop and were riding hell-bent for leather to overtake them.

"At least we'll have real food," Myrtle said while watching Petey rip out a handful of feathers. "I always feel better on a full stomach."

Fargo bent so his lips brushed her ear and whispered, "I always feel frisky."

Myrtle giggled.

Petey was so engrossed in his plucking, he didn't notice. He sneezed and said, "Darn feathers."

"Aren't you cute?" Myrtle said.

"Men aren't cute. Girls are."

"I didn't say you were a girl."

"You better not have."

"What's gotten into you all of a sudden? I give you a compliment and you bite my head off."

"I ain't no girl."

"You're just plain silly."

Fargo let them bicker. The madder Myrtle was at Petey, the easier it would be.

"It would be like me calling you handsome." Petey wouldn't let it drop.

"There's nothing wrong with that," Myrtle said. "And you're not a man yet."

"Stop bringing that up."

"Or what? You won't talk to me?" Myrtle laughed.

"I don't believe I will, no," Petey said, his feelings plainly hurt. "Not until you say you're sorry."

"Grow up."

"I mean it."

Fargo nipped their spat with a firm, "That's enough out of both of you. Try to get along until we're out of this mess."

"She started it," Petey said.

"Like hell," Myrtle rejoined.

"The next one who talks doesn't get to eat," Fargo said. That did it. They fell silent and Petey finished the plucking and gave the grouse to him. Fargo drew his toothpick and chopped off the head and the feet and slit the belly so the guts spilled out. He rigged a spit, sharpened a thick stick, and skewered the bird. The other two watched hungrily, Myrtle licking her nice lips. The aroma filled the clearing, making his mouth water. He was as hungry as they were.

Petey kept asking if it was done and finally it was. Fargo cut off a thick piece and placed it on his tin plate and gave the plate to Myrtle. She delicately picked up the meat and dropped it again, squealing, "It's hot!"

"It's fresh off the fire," Petey said. "What did you expect?"

"Know everything," Myrtle said.

Fargo gave a piece to Petey, then sliced off another, stuck the toothpick through the center, and ate it holding the knife hilt down so the meat wouldn't slide off. He chewed lustily while admiring the shapely contours of Myrtle's body. He liked the plan he had come up with. It promised to be entertaining.

They ate until they were fit to burst and there was little left of the grouse but bones. Fargo washed his meal down with piping-hot cups of black coffee. Myrtle had some, too. Petey, thankfully, didn't. It would have spoiled things if the boy stayed awake.

It helped, too, that the pair weren't talking to each other.

Fargo drank in silence, save for the howls and roars of the denizens of the Bitterroots. The predators were abroad in droves, lords of the darkness stalking prey in their nightly dance of death.

Fargo was secretly pleased when Petey stretched and yawned and announced that he was turning in. The boy looked hopefully at Myrtle but she didn't acknowledge the comment. Frowning, he spread out his blankets, curled on his side with his back to them, and said, "Good night."

"Sleep tight," Fargo said to amuse himself. He refilled his cup. Myrtle wanted more, too. He was happy to oblige her.

Petey commenced to snore. Nearby an owl hooted. Farther off a keening cry broke the night, sounding like an animal in dire torment.

Myrtle raised her head. "Was that a coyote?"

"A female fox," Fargo said. "Letting the male foxes know she's in the mood."

"Oh," Myrtle said, and her cheeks became pink. "I never think of animals doing that but they have to, don't they? Or there wouldn't be any animals."

"Doing what?" Fargo asked in feigned innocence.

"You know. *That*."

"I like that, myself," Fargo said, and grinned.

"Not enough to take me with you back at the farm," Myrtle said.

"I told you. I had to find him," Fargo said, and nodded at Petey.

"I suppose." Myrtle shrugged. "Oh well. I'm still alive so I suppose I should be grateful."

Fargo smiled and bent toward her and said with a suggestive lilt, "*How* grateful?"

34

Myrtle Adams looked at Fargo and said, "Oh." After a few seconds, her eyes widened slightly and she said "Oh!" again. A grin curved her red lips. "You can't have in mind what I think you have in mind."

"Why not?"

"We're in deep woods teeming with all sorts of wild beasts and with killers after us."

"The animals won't come near us and the killers won't catch up to us until tomorrow." If he let them, Fargo almost added.

"So you're saying it's perfectly safe?"

Fargo grinned. She was interested, he could tell. "Safe enough."

Myrtle sipped her coffee and stared into the crackling flames. At length she said, "It would be nice, I think. It would help me relax."

"We'd have to go off a ways."

She glanced at Petey. "Yes. We don't want to wake him. It would shock him silly, I bet."

"Whenever you want," Fargo said.

"I wanted to at the farm," Myrtle reminded him yet again. She gazed over her cup at his face. "God, you're handsome. Women must tell you that all the time."

"I don't pay much attention."

"Does this mean that after that is done you'll take me with you?"

"No," Fargo said. "It means I help you to relax so you can sleep tonight."

"You don't give an inch."

"I can't think about that now." Fargo sought to soften the sting. "I have other things on my mind."

"I know. Lazarus Wolfe. Those Blackfeet." Myrtle tilted her cup and then set it down and placed her hands on her legs. "Now is good, then. But you're absolutely sure it's safe?"

Fargo rose and pulled her to her feet. They stood chest to bosom and he said quietly, "If I wasn't, I wouldn't do this."

He molded her to him and his mouth to hers. She was stiff at first but she relaxed as the kiss went on and he explored her back and her bottom with his hands. He felt her melt into him.

When he broke the kiss she placed her forehead against him.

"You're a good kisser."

Fargo nipped her ear and licked her throat and his lips covered hers. He cupped a breast and she groaned deep in her throat. He forgot about Petey until the boy mumbled something in his sleep. Myrtle and he both glanced down.

"We'd better move off like you said."

Beyond the circle of firelight, under the spreading boughs of a tall pine, Fargo pressed her to him again. Raw desire washed over him. She was young and firm and easy on the eyes.

What she lacked in experience she more than made up for with her enthusiasm. They kissed for a long while, their tongues sliding and gliding. Fargo worked at the buttons on her dress and at last he bared her gorgeous mounds. He enfolded a nipple with his mouth and she shivered as if cold.

"Yessssss. I like that."

So did Fargo. He gave her other breast the same attention while hiking at her dress until it was bunched around her hips. She seemed not to notice until he placed a hand on her warm inner thigh. Then she shivered again.

"Mmmmmm. You sure do stoke a girl's fire."

Fargo caressed the silky sheen of her skin from her knee to her hip. She kissed his neck and his cheek and ran her fingers through his hair, knocking his hat off.

"God, I want you."

Fargo slid his hand between her legs and covered her nether mount. She was hot and moist. At the contact she bent her body into a bow and softly cooed. He parted her nether lips and slid his finger, eliciting a gasp of delight.

"There. Yes, there."

Fargo almost chuckled. He knew where it was. He touched her and she covered his face and neck with burning kisses.

"Don't stop."

Fargo wasn't about to. He slowly inserted his finger and she rose onto her toes and opened her mouth as if to scream but all she did was let out a long sigh of contentment. He stroked, and she bit him on the shoulder. Inwardly grinning, Fargo undid his belt buckle and lowered his gun belt to the grass. He went on stroking as he loosened his buckskin pants and felt them slide down to his knees. The cool night breeze brought goose bumps to his legs. He positioned her so her back was to the trunk, parted her thighs wide, and raised her high enough to impale her with his member. She gasped and clutched his arms.

"Yes! Oh! Yes."

Fargo pumped. Almost immediately she ground against him and closed her eyes and drenched him with her gush. He waited for her to subside, then commenced to rock on his heels.

"It feels so good," Myrtle breathed into his neck.

Fargo gripped her buttocks for extra leverage. He pumped in steady rhythm and she wrapped her legs around him and matched his vigor. Around them the dark was filled with yowls and cries. Fargo's ears were pricked for the slightest of sounds that might be a wild beast or a skulking enemy but he heard nothing to suggest they were in any danger. He went at her harder and faster, his need rising. So did hers. She wanted it as much as he did, as she demonstrated by gushing a second time, her body writhing in the ecstasy of release even as she locked her lips on his and sought to suck the breath from his body.

The explosion ripped out of Fargo's loins. It felt as if he was being torn in half, a delicious sensation that tingled every nerve.

They coasted to a sweaty stop, each of them breathing hard. Myrtle put her cheek to his chest and hugged him.

"Thank you. I wanted that so much."

"You weren't the only one."

She kissed his chin and traced his ear with her finger. "Now I can sleep like a log."

"Good," Fargo said, and hid his grin.

35

The eastern sky was brightening when Myrtle Adams sleepily stirred and slowly opened her eyes. She went to rise and glanced down at herself in alarm. "What in the world?" she blurted.

Fargo was sipping coffee. Across from him, Petey frowned and muttered his disapproval.

Myrtle raised her bound wrists and looked at them in amazement. "Who did this to me?"

"He did," Petey said.

Myrtle put her hands on the ground and pushed and sat up. She saw the rope around her ankles and said plaintively, "How could you?"

"I have a light touch," Fargo said.

"That's not what I meant." She looked at him, tears springing to her eyes. "How could you after we—" She stopped, glanced at Petey, and swallowed. "Tell me why, will you?"

"I told you last night," Fargo said. "The two of you are going on alone."

"Damn you," Myrtle said.

"It's for your own good."

"Double damn you," Myrtle said. "You wanted me so exhausted I wouldn't wake up when you tied me. That's it, isn't it?"

"I can't fight Wolfe and protect the two of you, both. I gave you your chance to go on your own and you wouldn't."

"I demand you untie me."

Fargo shook his head.

"Petey? Please," Myrtle said in appeal. "Surely you won't let him treat me this way."

"He says it's for the best," Petey said. "He says it's the only way to keep you from harm."

"*Please*," Myrtle said, and the tears poured. "I thought you liked me. If you do, you'll cut me free this instant."

"I do like you," Petey said. "And I don't want anything to happen to you."

"Then you won't?"

Petey shook his head, too.

"I'll scream, by God," Myrtle said. "I'll make such a ruckus, they'll hear me and know right where we are. What do you say to that?" she haughtily demanded of Fargo.

"I have some dirty socks in my saddlebags."

"What?"

"To gag you with."

"You wouldn't," Myrtle said, and uttered an unladylike comment. "What am I saying? Of course you would. And all for my own good."

"Now you savvy," Fargo said.

"Go—to—hell."

Fargo laughed. He set down his cup and stood. She didn't resist when he slipped his arms under her and carried her to the horses.

"Already saddled, I see."

"They'll be after us as soon as the sun is up," Fargo said. "You have to be gone by then." He swung her up and over her saddle, belly down. She squawked and swore and wriggled.

"Not this way. It's too uncomfortable. At least leave my legs free so I can sit the saddle."

"Petey will let you loose in a couple of miles."

"You don't trust me, do you? You think if you cut me free I'll give you trouble."

"I think you're a pain in the ass."

"I hate you," Myrtle said.

Fargo turned to the boy. "It's up to you to keep her safe."

"You can count on me," Petey said, and peeked past Fargo at Myrtle, who was still swearing and struggling. He whispered, "To tell you the truth, I think she's the prettiest girl I ever saw."

"Be strong. Don't let her talk you into cutting her free before I said to."

"I won't."

Fargo suspected the boy would be mush in her hands, so to speak. "Maybe I should gag her."

"There's no need," Petey assured him. "She can beg and whine but I won't listen."

"How about if she kisses you?"

"What?"

"Women have their ways," Fargo said.

"Do you really think she would? Kiss me, I mean? I've never had a girl kiss me before."

"It's hard to believe."

"What is?"

"That I was as young as you once, and as green behind the ears."

"Hold on," Petey said stiffly. "I'm not a child. And you taught me enough that you can't call me green."

"Yes," Fargo said. "I can. Teaching a pup a few tricks doesn't make it a grown dog." He gestured. "Up you go. Remember to fight shy of the high lines. We don't want them to spot you sneaking off."

"I tell you, I can do this," Petey insisted. He climbed on the sorrel and raised the reins. "Wait. I just had a thought."

Fargo looked up.

"What if something happens to you? They outnumber you ten to one."

"Forty to one," Fargo said.

"That's even worse." Petey leaned down. "Stall them if you have to but don't die doing it."

"I'm going to try not to."

"Why do this, anyhow? Why not come with us? We'll escape together."

"We've been all through this," Fargo said. "They'll catch us if I don't. Your only hope is if I can delay them."

"Here you are risking your hide for two people you hardly know. Why?"

"I don't have anything better to do."

"Can't you ever be serious? I like you, Mr. Fargo. I don't want you dead."

Fargo handed him the reins to the horse Myrtle was on. She glared.

"You're not going to answer me, are you?" Petey said.

Fargo was tired of being pestered. "Let's just say that Lazarus Wolfe has lived long enough. Now get the hell out of here." He smacked the sorrel and it jumped and Petey nearly dropped the reins. The boy looked back and grinned and gave a little wave. Myrtle flopped and glanced back and did more glaring.

Fargo waited until they were out of sight, then faced to the west. The outlaws and the war party would be coming soon, and the bright red of blood would mix with the morning dew.

36

It turned out he was wrong.

It was nearly an hour later when they showed. He was hidden midway up a slope dotted with boulders. There was a round in the Henry's chamber and the rifle's stock was to his shoulder. He took a bead on the first rider but he didn't shoot—it wasn't Lazarus Wolfe.

One by one they filed out of the trees. None were painted warriors. The entire gang came into the open. Only then did Fargo realize the Blackfeet weren't with them. He worried that the war party had circled and might be after the boy and Myrtle but he put it from his mind for the time being. First things first, as the old saying went.

Wolfe was the fourth rider. Fargo centered the sights on Wolfe's chest and curled his finger around the trigger. At that range he wouldn't miss. The scourge of the Bitterroots was about to meet his Maker. He held his breath to steady the Henry, and suddenly Wolfe dived headfirst from the saddle while simultaneously drawing and snapping two swift shots at the boulder. Fargo ducked, the whine of the ricochets loud in his ears. Somehow Wolfe had spotted him. Or, more likely, the gleam of sunlight on the brass receiver.

Hooves clattered. Fargo pushed to his feet and saw the first rider charging up the slope. He fired at the same instant the outlaw did. The man's forehead exploded and he pitched to the ground and tumbled to the bottom, his lifeless limbs flailing.

The rest of the gang scattered into the forest, Wolfe among them.

Fargo aimed at a rider who had twisted and was raising a revolver. The Henry bucked and the outlaw catapulted from his saddle. Fargo went to aim at another but they plunged into the vegetation and he didn't have a clear shot. With an oath he jerked the rifle down and raced up the slope. There was plenty of cover. He was over the rise and on the Ovaro before the outlaws could think to rush him. To draw them away from Petey and Myrtle he trotted to the south. He covered over half a mile before he glimpsed the Wolfe gang after him again. They were coming on fast, eager to take his life, Lazarus Wolfe in the lead.

Fargo grunted in satisfaction. He had accomplished the first part of his plan. Now all he had to do was stay alive to see it through. He pushed for another mile and then slowed to rest the Ovaro. The outlaws hadn't gained any so it was safe to do.

Fargo had some time to think. He was still concerned that the war party posed a threat to Petey and Myrtle, but there was another possibility. It could be that Lazarus Wolfe told them he didn't need their help. It could be that Wolfe and his men wanted to kill him themselves.

The timber inclined into a valley lush with high grass. Fargo went up the middle of the valley and around a bend to the far end and drew rein. If the outlaws stuck to his tracks, they'd be right out in the open. He climbed down and led the Ovaro into a cluster of pines and shucked the Henry from the scabbard.

A thick oak with a fork was the ideal vantage. He braced his left foot against a limb with his shoulder to another, and was ready.

They were a while in showing. By now their horses were winded and they came at a walk.

Fargo tucked the Henry to his cheek. It would be like plunking clay targets. He counted them as they came around the bend. Five, six, seven, and then no more. His puzzlement became alarm when the crackling of undergrowth revealed where Wolfe and the others had gotten to. Wolfe must have been suspicious of an ambush and looped through the woods to get ahead of him.

Fargo scrambled down. He went so fast, he scraped his left palm raw. Whirling, he was on the Ovaro before the outlaws coming up the valley spotted him. He reined deeper into the trees, and stopped. Shadowed figures were converging. Wolfe had sprung a clever little trap. Now the killers were on all sides.

Fargo shoved the Henry into the scabbard and drew the Colt. A flick of his boots, and he made his break. Someone yelled. A rifle barked. Pistols cracked. He swept around a thicket and suddenly Briscoll was in front of him. Briscoll pointed his revolver and thumbed back the hammer, a delay that cost him.

Fargo fired and a hole appeared between Briscoll's wide eyes. Then Fargo was past and the stallion crashed through the brush in headlong flight. More shots blasted. Slivers flew from a branch on Fargo's right. He answered, reined sharply aside, and was out of the circle of steel. Wolfe was angrily bellowing something about stopping him. Several more slugs sought his life.

Fargo fled. Or that was what he wanted them to think he was doing. He continued to the south, into country he had crossed on his way north. He'd always had a knack for recollecting landmarks and these were prominent: a granite peak split into a "V" and visible for many miles; a serrated ridge humped like the shell of a turtle; a series of cliffs that fringed a short plain.

Fargo drew rein. Coils of dust told him the outlaws were well back. They were taking their time, pacing their mounts, aware that so long as it didn't rain and wipe out the stallion's tracks, they could trail him to the end of the earth if they had to. He patted the Ovaro and unhooked his right boot from the stirrup and crooked his leg over the saddle.

His life depended on how well the next part went. He had it worked out in his head but to actually do it and survive was something else entirely. He was hungry yet he didn't open his saddlebags. Food might make him sluggish and every nerve must be razor taut.

The heat, the breeze, a fluttering butterfly, the world seemed so serene. It belied the violence that would explode as soon as the Wolfe gang spotted him. He stayed in the open so they would, and sure enough, the moment they came into sight, one of their number pointed and yelled and they broke into a gallop, thinking they had him.

Fargo lashed his reins. Maybe they did and maybe they didn't. In a couple of minutes he would find out.

37

The plain was broad and flat and offered no cover whatsoever. Wolfe's men hollered and whooped and a few revolvers banged.

Low over the saddle horn, Fargo focused on a particular spot—where the plain met the last of the cliffs. He was several hundred yards ahead of the outlaws when he reached it.

Suddenly the ground fell away. The end of the plain was itself a cliff. He reined sharply onto a rocky trail that would take him to the bottom. In a spray of stones and dust, the Ovaro slipped. For a few harrowing heartbeats Fargo thought they would go over but the sure-footed stallion recovered and pounded toward the bottom.

Fargo glanced up. He had a fair sense of when the outlaws would reach the edge. At a gallop they thundered to the end of the plain and the spot where the narrow trail began. Too many tried to go down the trail at once. They were moving so fast that only a few were able to haul on their reins and stop. In a flying jamb, half a dozen flew over the edge. Men screamed. Horses whinnied.

To Fargo it was as if they fell in spectacular slow motion. He saw the fear on the faces of the men, saw the horses kicking frantically, saw two of the animals turn upside down and the riders fall free. He reached the bottom only a few seconds before they hit. He swore the ground shook from the impact.

Flesh and bone crunched and split and bodies and heads burst and ruptured. Blood was everywhere. He sped for the next stretch of forest as above him the remaining outlaws cut loose with their rifles. The *thwack* and *zing* of lead was continuous until he was in the trees.

Fargo drew rein.

Lazarus Wolfe had not been among those who plummeted over the cliff. Now he was leading the remaining members of his gang down the trail, all of them with their rifles out and ready in case Fargo reappeared.

Fargo didn't. He rode on, racking his brain for another spot where the terrain would work in his favor.

The forest was bright with sunlight. Birds warbled and chirped and squirrels scampered in the trees. Occasionally he spooked deer and once a long-eared rabbit. He came to the grassy bank of a gurgling blue ribbon of water and once again stopped so the Ovaro could drink. The stallion dipped its muzzle and he was about to climb down and get a drink himself when upstream the brush rustled and another creature emerged with the same idea.

In reflex Fargo dropped his hand to his Colt but he didn't unlimber it. Against the behemoth that commenced to noisily drink, it would have little effect. The creature hadn't spotted him—yet. Quietly he reined around and into the woods and then swiftly back the way he had come. He didn't have to go far when he spied the outlaws, riding hard, more grimly determined than ever to catch him. He drew the Colt and fired one shot and wheeled the Ovaro. The outlaws immediately returned fire and gave chase.

His new gambit was fraught with peril. He galloped like mad for the stream and burst onto the bank only a few yards from the monster, which had stopped drinking and raised its huge head. The Ovaro cleared the bank and landed on the other side and was into the woods before the beast could react. It started to turn to come after him and then heard the outlaws.

Fargo drew rein yet again.

In their fierce passion to slay him the outlaws hurtled out of the vegetation and were at the stream before they realized the grizzly was there. The bear was on them in a fury. Claws and fangs rent and tore. It was a living dreadnought unleashed. A horse had its foreleg ripped off and crashed into the stream. Another had its neck opened. A rider's chest was shredded. Some of the others used their revolvers, which only made the grizzly madder.

Wolfe was shouting something. Several turned to flee. The grizzly was on them in surprisingly swift bounds for an animal so immense. Its roar froze a few of the horses. One man shrieked as a giant paw tore an arm from his body. Another had his face caved in. The outlaws scattered and the grizzly went after them.

Two had made it safely past the bear and were in the trees near Fargo. They had stopped and turned and were watching the lord of the wilds go after their companions.

"Jesus!" one exclaimed. "Did you see that?"

"About took Cliff's head off!" the other said.

"Do we help them?"

"Are you loco? You saw what that thing did."

"It's that scout, damn his hide. He led us right to it."

"Just like he did the cliff."

"God, I hate him."

"He's a tricky son of a bitch. I want him dead more than anything."

Fargo kneed the Ovaro. The pair was so intent on the bedlam they either didn't hear him or assumed he was one of them.

"Damn Wolfe, anyway," the skinniest outlaw said. "We should have stayed at the cabin."

"There was the girl, remember?"

"I wonder where she got to."

"I wouldn't have minded a few pokes of that," the other said. "I like young fluff."

"I have an idea," the skinny man said. "Let's light a shuck. We can slip away and leave these mountains and never look back."

"Wolfe might come after us."

"All he cares about right now is the scout. We'll never have a better chance."

"I don't know."

Fargo stopped. He held the Colt in front of him, the barrel pointed down, and said, "Gents."

Both twisted in surprise. The skinny one held a six-shooter, the other a rifle.

"You!" the skinny one blurted.

"What happened to the Blackfeet?" Fargo asked.

"What?"

"You heard me. Where did the war party get to?"

"What the hell does that matter?" the second man asked in bewilderment.

"Why didn't they join up with you?"

"Join up?" The skinny one barked like a dog. "Mister, we give them guns to leave us be, but that's all. They're red savages, for God's sake. We don't ever ride with them."

Fargo nodded. So that was it. Wolfe and his men were as bigoted as a lot of other whites. "I was curious."

They looked at one another.

"What now?" the skinny one said.

"We don't want any more of this," the second man threw in. "Let us go our way and you go yours."

"You've been trying to kill me for a couple of days now," Fargo said.

"So the answer is no?"

Fargo waited. They looked at one another and the skinny cutthroat swept his revolver up. Fargo shot him in the head. The second man fumbled with his rifle and bleated as Fargo sent a slug into his sternum. After the bodies stopped twitching Fargo replaced the spent cartridges and gigged the stallion toward the stream. He was through running.

It was time for the hunted to become the hunter.

Time to settle accounts with Lazarus Wolfe.

38

The cabin was quiet. The exhausted horses in the corral hung their heads in rest.

A fly buzzed Fargo and he almost raised his hand to swat at it but caught himself. The three men at the corral might see the movement. He was only a few feet into the fringe of woods.

The three were agitated and unhappy. They glanced repeatedly at the cabin door and spoke in low tones so as not to be heard.

Fargo remembered the names of two of the three, a beefy brute named Yardley and a broomstick with the unlikely name of Marion. The third man had a nervous tic in his left eye.

"I don't like it," Marion was saying. "I don't like how he's acting."

"He's mad that the scout got away," Yardley said.

"Got away, hell," Nervous Tic said. "We could have gone after him but Mr. High-and-Mighty didn't want to."

Marion glanced at the cabin and motioned. "Keep your damn voice down. Do you want him to hear you? He has ears like a cat's."

"What I want to know," Yardley said, "is where the others got to. That bear didn't get everybody who was left."

"They skedaddled, and I don't blame them," Nervous Tic

said. "Wolfe has been acting peculiar, even for him. He can't stand anyone getting the better of him and—"

"Hush!" Marion whispered.

Lazarus Wolfe was in the doorway, a half-empty whiskey bottle in his left hand, his right thumb in his gun belt. He took a careless swig and some of the whiskey dribbled down his chin. Wiping his mouth with his sleeve, he came toward the corral.

"Oh, hell," Nervous Tic croaked.

The three of them forced cheerful looks and Yardley said, "How is it going, boss?"

"How the hell do you think it's going?" Wolfe rejoined.

"I didn't mean nothing," Yardley said.

"The great Lazarus Wolfe gang," Wolfe mockingly spat. "Only you three jackasses left."

"No need for talk like that," Nervous Tic said. "We've stuck with you, haven't we?"

"It was them others who ran off," Marion said. "We've got more backbone than they did."

"Or you're more scared of me," Wolfe said.

"Why talk like that?" Nervous Tic said again. "I should think you'd be grateful to us for sticking."

"It's the scout you should be mad at," Marion said. "He made fools of all of us."

Wolfe swallowed more whiskey, his eyes embers of fury. "No one makes a fool of Lazarus Wolfe."

No one else said anything.

"I aim to find him. Before I'm done, he'll wish he was never born."

"Then how come we came back instead of going after him?" Yardley asked. "It's not like you to turn tail."

"What?" Wolfe said.

Marion took a step away from Yardley. "Oh God."

"What did you just say?" Wolfe said to Yardley.

"Nothing."

"You sure as hell did. You said I tucked tail. I heard you clear as day."

Sweat glistened on Yardley's face. "I didn't mean you did it because you were yellow. I meant you turned around and came back, is all."

"You don't know what in hell you're saying, do you?"

"Please, boss."

"I can't have a man ride with me, he thinks I'm a coward," Wolfe said.

"Don't put words in my mouth, goddamn it."

"How about I put lead?" Lazarus Wolfe said, and in a flash of lightning he drew and fired. The slug shattered Yardley's front teeth and sent blood spraying. Yardley staggered and clawed for his six-gun and Wolfe shot him again. Yardley crumpled, making hideous sounds deep in his throat, and violently convulsed before he went limp.

"God, no," Marion said.

Wolfe pointed the Smith & Wesson at him. "Do you know what I think? I think I should start over."

"Start over?" Marion repeated.

"With a whole new gang. You and Tilman, here, are as worthless as the rest."

"We stuck with you, damn it," Tilman said almost plaintively. "And this is how you'd repay us?"

"Yes," Wolfe said, and shot him in the face.

"God, God, God." Marion backed away, his hands up, palms out. "Please. I won't draw on you. Just let me ride off."

"You can draw if you want. It won't make a difference," Wolfe said.

"Just let me go."

"Here. I'll make it fair." Wolfe twirled the revolver into his holster.

"Fair, hell," Marion said. "I don't stand a prayer of beating you and you know it."

Wolfe chugged whiskey, and grinned. "Try anyway."

"Don't do this. It ain't right."

"Right?" Wolfe said, and laughed. "What the hell does right have to do with it?"

"It ain't fair, then," Marion said.

"You're as dumb as the rest. I'm Lazarus Wolfe. I do what I want when I want. None of you ever got that."

"We understood, all right," Marion said. "But we rode for you anyway. That should count for something."

"Not if you're in my boots, it doesn't," Wolfe said.

Marion glanced to either side as if contemplating his chances if he ran. "Let me go and I'll find others who'd like to ride with you. In no time you'll have your gang again."

"I can find them myself."

"I'm begging you."

"You're supposed to be on your knees for that," Wolfe said. "I don't see you on yours."

Marion dropped and clasped his hands. Tears trickled down his cheeks and he let out a sob. "See? I'm doing it the way you want. Now don't kill me."

Wolfe slowly drew his right Smith & Wesson and stepped in close. "Suck on this."

"What?"

"You heard me."

"I don't want to."

"You'll live a few seconds more."

"I still don't want to."

"Suit yourself," Wolfe said, and shot him in the temple.

As Marion collapsed, Wolfe chuckled and tilted the bottle to his mouth and emptied it. "Ahhhh," he said, and threw the bottle away.

Fargo drew his Colt and stepped into the clearing and stopped. He held the Colt low against his leg.

Lazarus Wolfe was about to take a step, and stiffened. Without turning his head he said, "It's you, ain't it?"

"It's me," Fargo said.

Wolfe looked over his shoulder. He stared at Fargo's gun hand. "Already out, I see."

"Same as yours."

"If it was a draw I'd beat you."

"Maybe," Fargo said. "Maybe not."

"How about we holster them and I turn and do it when you count to three?"

"Here and now," Fargo said.

"No one has ever given me half as much trouble as you. When you're dead I'll piss on your body."

"You have to do it first."

"There's that," Wolfe admitted. He smiled. "I am the quickest thing on two legs."

"Maybe," Fargo said. "Maybe not."

"Let's find out."

Lazarus Wolfe whirled and fired from the hip. Fargo was already in motion, throwing himself to the left. He felt a searing pain in his side. He fired in midair and Wolfe was jolted, fired again as Wolfe fired, fired a third time as he hit the ground and Wolfe was punched back but stayed on his feet and brought up both Smith & Wessons. Their muzzles were almost level when Fargo sent a slug into Wolfe's forehead.

Lazarus Wolfe swayed like an tree in a thunderstorm. He blinked, just once, as scarlet oozed from the bullet hole and down over his face. The Smith & Wessons fell from lifeless fingers and he smashed to the ground with his blank eyes fixed on the empty sky.

Skye Fargo stood. He raised his shirt and examined the wound. The slug had scoured him. It hurt like hell but he'd live. He reloaded, stared at the terror of the Bitterroots, and hastened to the Ovaro. He had a green boy and a young woman to find, and then he was going to plant root in a saloon and drink until he had booze coming out his ears.

He couldn't wait.

LOOKING FORWARD!
The following is the opening section of the next novel in the exciting *Trailsman* series from Signet:

TRAILSMAN #354
NEVADA NIGHT RIDERS

Comstock Lode, Virginia City, Nevada Territory, 1860— where warpath Indians, gold lust, and a doomsday prophet pile on the agony for Skye Fargo.

Skye Fargo hauled back on the reins, staring at the grisly abomination tied to the wheel of an abandoned freight wagon.

"Steady, old warhorse," he calmed his nervous stallion as it stutter-stepped away from the sickly-sweet smell of death. Fargo removed his hat to whack at the flies thickening the air.

Lips forming a grim slit through his cropped beard, the man some called the Trailsman studied the corpse bound to the wheel. The man had been shot so many times that Fargo couldn't count the bullet holes. But the shots had been carefully aimed so that death would not be quick. Both ears had been sliced off—a violent signature that Fargo recognized.

"Looks like Terrible Jack Slade's handiwork," he remarked to his black-and-white Ovaro. "This could get interesting."

It was Fargo's policy to bury any dead man he chanced upon so long as the deceased hadn't tried to kill him. But the mess on the wheel made his stomach churn. He booted his horse forward, eyes closed to slits against a merciless sun blazing in a hot blue sky. Virginia City, mountainside home of the gold-and-silver-rich Comstock Lode, lay straight ahead—a mining-town hellhole he would normally avoid like a cholera plague if a good friend hadn't asked for his help.

The majestic Sierra Nevada range of California rose high to the west, throwing its only spur into Nevada Territory. Fargo had been riding the federal road from Fort Churchill since sunup, pushing his luck. Three nomadic tribes—the Bannocks, the Shoshones and the Paiutes—had been on the scrap against white men since the Pyramid Lake Uprising, just last year, that slaughtered more than eighty whiteskins.

A half hour later Fargo rounded the shoulder of Mount Davidson and saw Virginia City spread out before him. It looked surprisingly like a real town complete with false fronts and plank-board walkways. The Comstock lay at the foot of the town in Washoe Valley. Fargo had just reached the outskirts of town when an astonishing sight made him rein in: about a dozen women came running along Center Street, naked as newborns.

Fargo was pleased but not baffled: the infamous "running of the whores" was a daily ritual in Virginia City to advertise the carnal wares and get the miners all het up. He nudged the Ovaro aside to let them pass.

"Hey, Buckskins!" called out a buxom redhead as the girls

flew past. "It's on the house for you and those dreamy blue eyes. Ask for Trudy at the Gold Room."

"A stallion riding a stallion!" chimed in a petite blonde with a corn-silk bush. "Ask for Jenny at the Wicked Sisters saloon. I'll climb all over you."

Fargo doffed his hat. He knew that most men—himself definitely included—needed to cut the buck now and then. But these gold grubbers on the Comstock didn't just raise hell—they *tilted* it a few feet.

Fargo heard bells clanging from the Washoe, the steam skips that took men deep down into the stopes, or mine chambers, where gold and silver were extracted from the veins. Trees were scarce and signs all over town warned WATCH YOUR LUMBER!!! Evidently the signs weren't much use because Fargo could see that boards were missing everywhere.

He spotted a small cubbyhole office with the words VIRGINIA CITY JAIL painted on the door. Fargo reined left, swung a long leg over the cantle, and landed light as a cat. He wrapped the reins around a hitch-rack fronting the building and pulled his brass-framed Henry rifle from its saddle scabbard. Then he went inside.

The moment he entered Fargo saw a sturdy, earnest-looking young man seated at a battered kneehole desk sorting through a stack of wanted dodgers. He had a strong jaw and a part in his hair straight as a pike.

"Marshal Jimmy Helzer?" Fargo asked.

"Right down to the ground," the lawman confirmed, his tone friendly but guarded. "Friend or foe? From the look of you, I hope it's friend."

Fargo laughed. "Any kid brother of Captain Pete Helzer is definitely my friend."

Jimmy's eyes brightened and he stood up, offering his hand. "Ah, hell, I should have known you, Mr. Fargo. Wearing buckskins, carrying a brass-frame Henry, that Arkansas toothpick in your boot. And I'll bet you rode in on a first-rate Ovaro. Pete told me you were riding dispatches between Sacramento and Fort Churchill."

"That's the way of it," Fargo confirmed.

Jimmy's eyes clouded with suspicion. "Say, did Pete send you up here because he thinks I can't handle this job?"

Fargo chuckled. "Son, does your mother know you're out? *No* one man can handle this job. I read in a San Francisco newspaper that the Comstock produced more wealth in the past year than the entire nation. All that color ups the ante on violence. You need at least five deputies. Hell, last time I was here Virginia City was just an empty mountainside with one steep mule path."

"Things change fast in a boom. Now we have thirteen thousand people, forty stores, twenty-five saloons and one hundred well-built homes."

Jimmy pointed Fargo to a chair and perched on one corner of the desk. "We've got more than a few pick-and-shovel millionaires running around town. But for every man who strikes a bonanza, twenty more go bust and get desperate. And the ones who do strike a lode are lucky to hang on to their claims."

"These new corporation fellows, right?"

"Yep. Last year, one of those slickers from New York got a man named Jay Kajewski tanked and bought his claim for five thousand dollars. It has since produced two million dollars in gold. Men who won't sell meet with 'accidents.'"

None of this was news to Fargo. Out on the frontier nothing was cheaper than a human life. Killing didn't carry the stigma it did back east. Most murders weren't even investigated or ended in acquittals. A man was far more likely to hang for horse theft than for murder.

"Yours is no job for a featherbed soldier," Fargo agreed.

"I'm a fair-to-middling hand with firearms," Jimmy added. "But this town is crammed with gun-handy murderers and shakedown artists hungry for easy money. And these prospectors and miners are a strange, half-civilized bunch. We've had two shooting affrays already today and it's barely past noon. When I tried to find witnesses everybody suddenly went blind."

"Boomers," Fargo said, "are the same everywhere—profit quick and move on. All they've ever known of 'law' is badge-happy bullies, so they don't trust it. And it can't help that you have Terrible Jack Slade to wrangle."

Jimmy looked uneasy. "You know him?"

"He doesn't exactly stand in thick with me, but I know him and I'm glad we've never locked horns. He could make Satan himself step off the sidewalk."

"I won't lie to you, Mr. Fargo. The man fair gives me the fidgets. He's crazy as a shitepoke as soon as he gets a couple under his belt—and as dangerous as a sore-tailed bear."

"Turns into a kill-crazy marauder," Fargo agreed. "I take it you know about the . . . thing tied to a wagon wheel south of town?"

Jimmy nodded, worry suddenly molding his young face. "Slade's work, all right. I just don't know how to handle him."

"Neither do I so I just let him be. When he's sober he's

friendly and mannerly—hell, even gentle. But firewater transforms him. Far as I know, though, he never bothers decent people."

"No. And even though I suspect him of six killings since he got here, every damn one *needed* killing. Rafe Jennings, the body you saw, was wanted for raping and killing a thirteen-year-old Chinese girl."

"Glad I didn't bury him," Fargo said.

Jimmy chewed on his lower lip. "Pete told me this job is too much for me. Wants me to go back to farming in Iowa. I'm from a village called May Bee. Only criminal I know of back there was a barn burner."

"You're free, white, and twenty-one—that's your decision, not Pete's. But he told me you were once a sheriff in Placerville."

"Constable, actually."

"If it pounds nails it's a hammer. By any name, a man has to use his fists and his wits to keep a Sierra mining camp in line. And the Comstock is worse."

"Well . . ."

"Jimmy, law can't be perfect in a hellhole like this. If you push too hard, you'll be murdered. Say, do you like a stiff belt now and then?"

Jimmy looked embarrassed. "Whiskey gives me dyspepsia. I like a cold beer though."

Fargo pushed to his feet. "I need to cut the trail dust. What's the best saloon in town?"

"Well, the Wicked Sisters is the cleanest. It's on the south side of Center Street—long wooden awning out front."

"Tell you what," Fargo said. "I have to put up my horse, so why don't you meet me in twenty minutes or so at the saloon? I'll stand you to a drink and we'll palaver a little more about this Sodom."

"Sure," Jimmy said. "I could use—"

Outside, a crackling volley of gunfire erupted. Jimmy didn't look the least bit surprised.

"Celebration fire," he remarked. "Some lucky bastard just hit pay dirt. He'll be even luckier if he can hang on to it."

Fargo trotted his stallion down wide and dusty Center Street, amazed at how Virginia City had mushroomed since he had last been here two years earlier. He was astounded to see a small public library, although the building stood empty. At the east end of town he spotted a combination smithy and livery barn.

As he tugged rein and crossed the hoof-packed yard, he heard the piercing ring of a hammer on an anvil. Fargo lit down and led the Ovaro inside, spotting a heavyset man with hairy hands shaping a horseshoe on the anvil.

"What can I do you for?" he greeted Fargo, studying the Ovaro's impressive muscle formation. "Finest-looking horse I've seen in a long time."

"He'll do to take along," Fargo agreed. "As soon as you can, would you give him a feed and a rubdown? And can you board him for a few days?"

"Be a pleasure. Prices are steep, though. Dollar a day."

Fargo nodded. That price was indeed steep, but he expected it in a thriving gold town. He stripped the saddle loose and threw it over a saddle rack, hanging his bridle over the horn.

After a quick washup at the pump in the yard, Fargo headed down the plank walkway toward the Wicked Sisters saloon. Along the way drunk, wild-eyed miners and prospectors, some armed like Wells Fargo guards, staggered out of saloons, eyes seeking trouble. But one look at Fargo's granite-chiseled, sun-bronzed face and fearless gaze made them veer away from him.

Fargo slapped open the slatted batwings of the Wicked Sisters and entered a crowded, smoke-hazed, raucous barroom. A hurdy-gurdy machine sent out its mechanical version of music, produced by the friction of a rosined wheel on the strings. Fargo noticed that some of the men, clothes stained red with ore, wore knuckle-dusters—loops of heavy, shaped brass wrapped around their hands. Drinking jewelry, soldiers called them, and Fargo knew a solid blow could kill or cripple a man.

He spotted Jimmy at the long counter of raw milled boards. The kid wasn't too green, Fargo realized—he was standing with his back to a wall and he could see anyone who came in.

"Brother," Fargo greeted him, "you've chosen a hard way to make thirty dollars a month and found."

"Oh, it's a mite more than that. I get a buck and a half for every drunk I manage to buffalo and jug."

A barkeep wearing sleeve garters and a Mormon wreath beard had to lean close so he could hear them.

"Skye Fargo, meet Tim Bowman," Jimmy said. "Best bar dog on the Comstock."

"*The* Skye Fargo?" Bowman asked. "The jasper the newspapers claim cleaned out that gang in South Pass?"

"A newspaperman," Fargo opined, "is a little old lady of both sexes."

Bowman looked apologetic. "I'm required by my employers to notify all new customers: no folding money. Gold and pure silver are all that spend here." He leaned in even closer. "But I'll also accept good nails—there's a serious shortage."

Fargo planked a gold cartwheel. "A shot of whiskey for me and a barley pop for the boy marshal here."

"It's lousy wagon-yard whiskey," Bowman warned. "The red sons have choked off the only supply routes, so we distill our own."

Privately, Fargo suspected the free-ranging tribes in this area had much larger, bloodier ambitions than harassing freighters.

"It's a pisser," Jimmy complained. "We're being slowly choked off. Three months ago you could get any luxury you wanted in this town, even tins of caviar and oysters. And Fort Churchill is only about four hours' ride southeast of here."

"They can't help anybody right now," Fargo said. "Between desertion, disease and combat casualties almost half of Pete's troop is hors de combat."

Jimmy nodded. "Some of those deserters you mentioned are here in Virginia City looking for color. I just got a telegram from Pete. The entire fort has only thirty-five effectives, and they can't patrol—they're needed for force protection from hostiles."

"Yeah, and Camp Floyd and Fort Bridger are too far east in the Nevada Territory. Troops would have to cross the Black Rock Desert. The Paiutes and Shoshones are strong now and they'd cut the troops down."

Fargo tossed back the rotgut and tears immediately filmed his eyes as a fiery pit replaced his stomach. "Every word you said is gospel, Jimmy, but before you can organize the louts and hard tails in *this* town to fend off Indians you'll have to somehow gain control of the worst elements among the residents."

As if in response to Fargo's remark, the entire saloon abruptly fell silent, even the hurdy-gurdy. Fargo watched a dime-a-dance girl's face turn chalk white as she stared at someone outside. The doors meowed inward and a tall, powerfully built man dressed all in black broadcloth strolled in.

"He's on a tear," Jimmy groaned. "Looks mad as a March hare."

Fargo took in the handsome man's silver concho belt, the tied-down Remingtons with walnut grips—and the disgusting necklace of dried, blackened human ears.

"You ignorant bogtrotters!" Terrible Jack Slade said in a voice strong enough to fill a canyon. "Don't you see the Grim Reaper standing before you now?"

The saloon had gone as silent as a graveyard at midnight. Fargo couldn't spot one man with the courage to meet Slade's intense black eyes. Casually, the Trailsman thumbed the riding thong from the hammer of his Colt. But he knew exactly who—and what—Slade was, and Fargo couldn't help an icy nervousness along his spine.

Slade chuckled, his face contorted from the controlled insanity within him. "All right, sheeple, *don't* believe the harbinger of doom. One week from today, anh? Midnight next Wednesday—a beast will rise from the bowels of the earth. And if you are still here, you will *all* be eaten alive!"